Nigel stared up at her, his lips pulled in a tight line. He looked angry.

So Callie couldn't have been more startled when he suddenly got to his feet, stepped in front of her and slipped his fingers into her hair. "Do you know how many days I wondered if you would come back to me?" he asked, his hot breath fanning her face. "Do you know how many times I wished you hadn't walked out on me?"

Callie couldn't speak. All she could register was the furious pounding of her heart as she wondered if Nigel was going to kiss her.

Did she want that?

The fact that her body felt more alive than ever made it clear that she *did* want it.

"I wanted to do this so many times," he said, trailing one finger down her cheek, creating a path of fire. "But you never gave me the chance. Because you never came back."

Callie couldn't speak. Suddenly, desire was pulsing through her veins.

Nigel's mouth came down on hers, hard. Her body erupted in an immediate firestorm of passion. He kissed her with an urgent need that matched all the raging sensations inside of her. Kissing Nigel, it was as though no time had passed at all.

Books by Kayla Perrin

Kimani Romance

Island Fantasy
Freefall to Desire
Taste of Desire
Always in My Heart

KAYLA PERRIN

has been writing since the age of thirteen and once entertained the idea of becoming a teacher. Instead, she has become a *USA TODAY* and *Essence* bestselling author of dozens of mainstream and romance novels, and has been recognized for her talent, including twice winning Romance Writers of America's Top Ten Favorite Books of the Year Award. She has also won the Career Achievement Award for multicultural romance from *RT Book Reviews*. Kayla lives with her daughter in Ontario, Canada. Visit Kayla at www.kaylaperrin.com.

Always
In My Heart

Kayla Perrin

KIMANI™
ROMANCE

KIMANI PRESS™

Recycling programs
for this product may
not exist in your area.

ISBN-13: 978-0-373-86256-6

ALWAYS IN MY HEART

Copyright © 2012 by Kayla Perrin

www.kimanipress.com

Printed in U.S.A.

Dear Reader,

Blood is thicker than water—isn't it? Then why are familial relationships often so complicated? Especially the sibling relationship?

Rivalries that begin in childhood, failed expectations… these are just a couple of the issues that brothers and sisters deal with. And when the siblings are of the same gender, the conflicts are even greater. I think we can all relate!

The subject matter is fascinating, and it's why I decided to write about the Hart sisters. Callie, Natalie and Deanna haven't had the easiest relationship. Estranged for years, they are brought back together when their aunt dies—the woman who raised them. Suddenly they realize that, no matter what happens, the ties that bind are greater than the ones that pull us apart. Especially when they learn there is more to their mother's disappearance than they ever imagined.

I'm thrilled to present the Harts in Love series to you! Enjoy!

For my father,
Lenworth Hugh Perrin.

A true man of honor and integrity.
One who was always there for his children,
and always there for his wife.
A man who taught me that through hard work
I could accomplish anything.

I never expected to lose you so soon,
and I hope that you know
of all the fathers in the world,
I'm glad God blessed me with you.

I love you, Dad.
You are always in my heart.

Chapter 1

Callie Hart was numb.

As the airport limousine came to a stop, all she registered was the ominously dark sky and the large, steady drops of rain that had been falling since she had arrived at Cleveland Hopkins International Airport. The rain mirrored the tears that had been falling from her eyes ever since she had heard the news.

Her aunt was dead.

The tragic news had been hard for her to bear. Auntie Jean had been more than simply an aunt to her. She had been a mother. Ever since the day twenty-three years ago when her own mother had dropped off her and her two sisters at their aunt's place and promised to be back, Auntie Jean had become their true mother.

"Mom, I think we're here."

At the sound of the voice, Callie glanced to her right. Kwame, her nine-year-old son, was looking at her with concern. His eyes were dry. He hadn't known his great-aunt well though he'd seen her a handful of times. Therefore he didn't have the chance to feel an emotional attachment to the truly amazing woman Callie had known and loved.

Callie offered Kwame a brave smile, noting that the driver had already exited the car and had the trunk open. After booking their flight, Callie's next call had been to arrange for a private car service. The last thing she wanted was to get to the airport and have to wait on a regular taxi in her distressed state of mind.

Now, Callie looked out at the church her aunt had attended for eons. Once, Callie had imagined being married in this church. Instead, she was here to say goodbye to someone she loved.

Ten years. In ten long years, she hadn't been back to Cleveland, for which she suddenly felt enormous guilt.

At the time, she had left for a reason that had seemed legitimate, and had stayed away all these years for the same reason. Now, in the wake of what had happened to her aunt—as well as her own brush with death days earlier—her reason suddenly seemed unsubstantial. She had lost years with her family. Time she was all too aware she would never get back.

"Mom, is that a hearse?"

At the question, Callie's eyes went forward. Indeed, the limo had parked behind the hearse.

Callie swallowed hard, the sight making it clear that she wasn't in the middle of a nightmare.

Callie was about to reach for the door handle with her good hand when it suddenly opened. "Ma'am," the driver said. He held an enormous black umbrella over the door to shield them from the rain.

As Callie stepped out of the car, she saw her luggage on the sidewalk. It suddenly hit her that she couldn't head into the church with her suitcases. She would need them taken to the house.

"Norman, right?" Callie said.

"Yes, ma'am."

"Is there any possible way you can wait for me?" Callie asked him. "I didn't think of it until now, but we're here for a funeral, and…if you can stick around, I'll make it worth your while." Pausing, Callie considered how much he was charging for the trip from the airport. "If you're willing to be my driver for the next few hours or so, I'll offer you five times what I'm already paying you."

The man's blue eyes widened, indicating his surprised pleasure, before he resumed his business composure. "I'm happy to accept your offer. I'm yours for as long as you need me."

"Excellent. If you wouldn't mind putting the luggage back into the trunk, that would be great."

"Of course. Just let me get you both into the church."

Norman walked with Callie and Kwame to the church's doors, making sure they got inside without getting soaked. It was late May, and the spring shower was in full force.

"Thank you, Norman," Callie said.

Norman, in his mid-fifties with salt-and-pepper hair, nodded. Then he said, "I'm sorry for your loss."

The words made Callie's breath catch in her chest. It hit her once more that she would never see Auntie Jean again.

As though Kwame sensed that she needed strength, he took her hand. Callie gripped it and ascended the few steps that led toward the sanctuary. She couldn't help thinking that Kwame was turning from a boy into a young man. And she couldn't have been prouder of him. He was mostly respectful, though he wasn't perfect. He'd had a rebellious spell just last year, which Callie attributed to her breakup with Philip, her last boyfriend. He'd been a father figure to Kwame, and her son had been crushed to lose him.

Kwame had blossomed with Philip around, and Callie then realized what her son needed all along.

The very thought had Callie's heart constricting. She had thought of pretty much nothing else ever since being admitted to the hospital after her car crash, and the news of her aunt's death two days later had only made her thoughts more serious.

She had come back to Cleveland after ten years for her aunt, but also for another reason. To rectify a wrong.

"How does your arm feel?" Kwame asked.

"It's okay," Callie said. The pain in her shoulder was nothing compared to the pain in her heart.

As she and Kwame reached the top step, two older men who were standing there handed her a funeral program. Callie took it, saw the smiling picture of her aunt on the cover, and fresh tears filled her eyes.

And then she walked down the aisle of the church. The coffin was at the front, and open. She suddenly wondered if she should let Kwame see Auntie Jean like that, or if she should spare him the experience. But sadly, death was a part of life, and she knew she couldn't shield her son from that reality forever.

A head in the front pew turned. And then Callie was staring into the eyes of her sister, Deanna. Callie wasn't sure how either of her sisters would react to her after all these years, but Deanna immediately got to her feet and started down the aisle toward her. As if no time had passed, she moved toward her with open arms and wrapped her in an embrace.

"Callie," she said, a little sob escaping her. "It's so good to see you."

Callie drew strength from Deanna's hug. "It's good to see you, too."

Funny how it sometimes took death to bring people together. Because while Callie hadn't had a particular beef with either of her sisters, being forced into the middle of an ugly conflict between Deanna and Natalie had led to her being estranged from both of them.

Deanna turned her attention to Kwame. "And you must be Kwame. I'm your aunt. Aunt Deanna."

"Hi," Kwame said, his voice faint. He was normally an outgoing kid, but he was always shy when meeting people for the first time.

"You're very handsome," Deanna said, offering him a smile.

"Thanks." He paused, then said, "I've seen you on TV. My mother showed me one of your music videos."

"She did, did she?"

Kwame nodded. "It was a couple years ago. When I was seven. I like your music."

"Well, that's good to hear." Deanna ran her hand over his head affectionately.

"Is Natalie here?" Callie asked, knowing this was a touchy subject.

"Yeah. Like you, she couldn't make it before today. She just arrived a little while ago. We've said hi, but not much else."

Callie nodded. "Where is she?"

"Downstairs in the bathroom. She was…" Deanna paused, swallowed. "A wreck."

"Yeah," Callie said softly, knowing the feeling. Deanna's own eyes were red and puffy, indicating that she had cried a lot of tears. But it was clear she was trying to keep it together now.

Callie took a good, long look at Deanna. Her sister had definitely changed in ten years. Her face was still slim, but her body had filled out, turning her from a skinny teen into a woman. Ten years ago, Deanna had liked wearing her hair shoulder length, but now it was cut into a short style and combed back from her face, letting her beauty show.

"Uncle Dave said you'd been in a car crash." Deanna's eyes swept over her, assessing her injuries. "But he said you told him it wasn't serious. Yet you're wearing a sling, and you've got a big bandage on your head. It looks like you were pretty hurt."

"I'll be fine," Callie said.

Deanna looked at Kwame. "But he was unhurt?"

"Thank God."

Deanna sighed softly. "Yes, thank God. I'm so glad you're both here."

As silence passed between them, Callie knew that Deanna was thinking the accident could have been much worse. That it could have taken both her and Kwame's lives.

"Why don't you come with me for a minute?" Deanna said, wrapping an arm around Kwame's shoulders. "I'll introduce you to some other family members."

"Okay."

As Deanna began to walk with Kwame, she gave Callie a look, then jerked her head ever-so-slightly toward the front of the church. She was letting her know that this was a good time to go and pay her final respects to their aunt.

Callie moved forward, her legs feeling like lead as she made her way to the polished mahogany casket. Floral arrangements filled the front of the church. Callie saw the wreath she was certain she had ordered, the one that read "Beloved Mother" and was brightly colored, made up of pink, orange, yellow and lime-colored flowers.

Also at the front of the church were pictures of Auntie Jean in happier times. She had been so full of life, it seemed impossible that her life had been cut down at fifty-seven from a brain aneurysm.

Callie stepped up to the coffin and looked down at her aunt. Tears began to fall again. She was comforted only by the fact that Auntie Jean looked peaceful.

When she felt the arms encircle her waist, Callie looked to her right. Kwame was there at her side, being there for her once more, offering her his strength.

"This is your great-aunt, honey," Callie said. "You met her a few times when she came to Florida to see us, but the last time was three years ago." *Way too long.*

"She was beautiful," Kwame said.

"Yes, she was," Callie said, and leaned her head down to touch Kwame's, as her shoulder injury prevented her from hugging him properly.

"Callie?"

At the sound of the tentative female voice behind her, Callie turned. Her youngest sister, Natalie, stood a few feet away. A sob escaping her lips, Natalie moved forward, and the two sisters embraced.

"I can't believe it's you," Natalie said. "It's been so long."

"I know. I just wish it wasn't under these circumstances that we are seeing each other."

Natalie nodded. She shot a brief glance over her shoulder in Deanna's direction, and Callie couldn't help wondering if her two sisters were going to continue their feuding.

"And what happened to you? I hear—and see—that you were in a car accident."

"I'll tell you all about it later," Callie said. She glanced beyond Natalie to where her uncle was sitting on a pew, looking grief stricken. "But I've got to say hi to Uncle Dave, and the rest of the family."

"Yes, of course."

Uncle Dave stood as she approached him. He seemed frail, weak with sorrow. He had married their aunt two years after they'd gone to live with her, and he'd been the only father they'd ever known.

"Uncle Dave," Callie said, wrapping her good arm around him. She felt his frame shudder with a sob.

"Thank you for coming," he said.

"Of course I would come," Callie said, again feeling guilt.

Because there was no *of course* about it, at least not where Uncle Dave was concerned. How could he have been certain that she would come when she had so effortlessly put Cleveland in her rearview mirror? Yes, she'd been in touch with Auntie Jean and Uncle Dave, but less and less over the years, and she had seen them only when they'd come to Florida to visit.

"I'm sorry," Callie whispered. It was all she could say. Because no excuse she gave to justify her absence all these years was going to be substantial enough.

But she was here now, ready to start fresh.

The funeral service was extremely moving, resulting in tears flowing from everyone's eyes. Uncle Dave, whom Callie had only known to be strong, was inconsolable as the pallbearers took his wife's coffin from the church.

The rain continued to fall, making the cemetery burial a soggy mess, but no one was concerned about the discomfort. All they wished was that Jean Henry could be back with them.

Callie had heard that rain was a blessing, and she only hoped that the spring downpour was a sign that Auntie Jean had ascended to heaven to be with her maker.

All Callie really wanted to do after the graveside service was head back to her old home and sleep for a few hours, but Uncle Dave's brothers and sisters were hosting a repast for all the mourners at the house. Callie had no choice but to participate.

The extended family and friends had made all kinds of

food and desserts, and after a few hours of solemn mourning, many people were now smiling and laughing as they remembered Auntie Jean. Callie knew her aunt would want it this way, but she wasn't yet ready to smile.

"Do you want something to drink, Mom?" Kwame asked.

Callie was sitting on a love seat in the living room with her son, still feeling numb despite the chatter and activity around her. She wasn't hungry at all, and had already refused his offer to get her food. She was about to tell him that she didn't need anything to drink, but thought better of it. Her son was trying to take care of her, something she appreciated.

"You know what? I wouldn't mind some tea."

Kwame gave her a smile, and got up from the love seat. About ten seconds after he went into the kitchen, Deanna came into the living room and took the vacant seat beside her.

For a long moment, they were silent. Then Deanna sighed and said, "You know what I was kind of thinking today? Hoping…"

She didn't finish her statement, but the lump that lodged in Callie's throat said she knew what she'd been about to say. And while she had wanted to keep her mind from going there, she'd also had the same fleeting thought.

"Our mother," Callie concluded. "You thought she might show up."

"Auntie Jean *is* her sister, after all."

Callie looked forward, her jaw tightening. She hated thinking about their mother. It always brought her down. Twenty-three years ago, she had waited by the window in this very house, day and night, for their mother to return, as she'd promised.

She never had.

"Maybe she couldn't come," Callie said. "I mean, maybe…"

Deanna's eyes closed tightly, even though Callie didn't finish her statement. But with all this time that had passed, how could either of them ignore the possibility that their mother could be dead?

Certainly, for their aunt to have died, Miriam Hart would have made it to the funeral if she could have.

So many questions where their mother was concerned, yet no answers.

Callie didn't want to think about their mother anymore, so she said, "I know it's been a busy day, and you and Natalie haven't really had a chance to talk. But I'm wondering… do you think you're going to patch things up?"

"Ten years have passed," Deanna said.

"That doesn't answer the question."

"I know… What I'm saying is, ten years have passed. I'm willing to put the past in the past."

Callie raised an eyebrow. "Are you sure about that?"

Deanna sighed softly. "I'm not saying it's going to be easy, but if Auntie Jean's passing hasn't made it clear that holding grudges is pointless…"

There had been a lot going on today, but Callie had noticed that Natalie was making sure to avoid Deanna. The funeral and the aftermath was allowing both of them to be busy and completely avoid each other.

"You're going to have to try to talk to her soon then," Callie said. "Because she might be getting on a plane and heading back to Texas before we know it. Isn't her husband's team in the NBA finals? She'll want to be there to support him."

"You haven't heard?" Deanna asked.

"Heard what?"

"Natalie and Vance split up. At least, that's the gossip. You never know if it's true or not, but I did notice she wasn't wearing a wedding band."

Callie narrowed her eyes. She hadn't noticed. All she knew—from her aunt and uncle and from various news clips about four years earlier—was that Natalie had married a basketball star who played for the San Antonio Badgers. She didn't keep up with celebrity gossip, and hadn't heard anything about a split.

"I had no clue," Callie said.

"The word is, Vance couldn't be faithful. The latest news is that they just split a few weeks ago."

Perhaps that explained why Natalie seemed completely inconsolable. She had been crying almost constantly, and had excused herself to head upstairs and lie down once they'd gotten back to the house.

"Wow, that's horrible," Callie commented.

"Yeah," Deanna said softly. She paused. "When I first heard, I couldn't help thinking that she got what she deserved. After what she did to me... But seeing her today, seeing how much pain she's in...well, all I could do was feel pity."

"All the more reason to let her know that you're willing to put the past behind you," Callie pointed out. "Men may come into our lives for a season, but we're blood. We never should have drifted apart."

"I hear you," Deanna said.

One of them would have to make the first move. If she had to, Callie would do it on their behalf, once all the visitors had left the house.

In the grand scheme of things, how stupid had the whole incident been. Ten years they had been out of each other's lives, and for what? Natalie had seduced Deanna's boyfriend, which had been a horrible thing to do, and the rift between Natalie and Deanna had begun.

Callie remembered getting into the middle of the conflict, trying to help both of her sisters see the light. But they'd been so absorbed in their own differences and unable to reconcile, and had gotten mad at Callie for not understanding that the other sister was at fault.

Having had a close friend who had died after a severe

police beating at the time, Callie grew tired of her younger sisters' squabble. There were far more important things to deal with in the world.

Like the fact that she'd been pregnant and confused, and had felt alone.

"Speaking of men coming into our lives for a season," Deanna began, "guess who dropped by the funeral home last night?"

"I don't know," Callie said, shrugging. Then she guessed the name of the guy Deanna and Natalie had become estranged over. "Marvin?"

"No, not Marvin, thank God. Nigel."

Nigel! At the sound of his name, Callie's heart slammed against her rib cage. Nigel had come to pay his respects to Auntie Jean?

Why was she surprised? Auntie Jean had adored him when they were together, and he her. One of the reasons Callie had stayed away and not told her family the entire truth was because she couldn't trust that they wouldn't let her secret slip to Nigel.

"He—he did?" Callie asked, her voice a croak.

"Mmm-hmm."

Good Lord, was he going to drop by the house today? Callie suddenly looked toward the front door, as if he might show up at any moment.

"Did you—you talk to him?" Callie asked, then swallowed.

"Briefly. He said he came in to pay respects to Uncle Dave and the family. He offered us condolences, said how sorry he was for our loss, then he left."

Did he ask about me? That was the next question on Callie's lips, but somehow she stopped herself from asking it. As if she even had the right to think that after what she'd done.

Her stomach clenched, knowing that what she had planned to do was going to be excruciatingly hard. But it had to be done. As difficult as it would be to face Nigel, she knew that she had to.

She only hoped that when she dropped her doozy of a bombshell on him, he didn't hate her forever.

Chapter 2

"Detective Williams?"

Nigel Williams sat up straight when he heard the soft voice on the other end of the line. Was this the call he had been waiting for?

"Yes," he said. "This is Detective Williams."

"I hear you wanted to talk to me."

"Dominiqua?"

"Yes," came the low reply.

The murder victim's girlfriend. *Thank God.* "You were there last night? When Garrett was shot?"

"Yes." The girl began to cry.

"I need you to come in to the station," Nigel said. "So we can talk about what happened."

"I—I'm scared. If I talk to you, people will find out. And…"

Her voice trailed off, but her sentiment was clear. She

was afraid to talk, because of the code on the streets—never snitch.

It was an all-too-common conundrum. People were afraid to come forth with information for fear of retaliation against them. But the catch-22 was that when people didn't come forward to report the bad guys, the bad guys were still on the streets to hurt other people.

"I can come to you," Nigel offered. "Just tell me—"

"No! No cops. I can't be seen talking to a cop—"

"If you saw what happened, if you have information, it's important that you tell me," Nigel said, speaking as gently as possible. "We can figure out a spot to meet that will be safe for you."

"I'm sorry," Dominiqua said. "I—I can't."

And then she hung up.

Nigel heard the dial tone, and groaned in frustration as he replaced the phone to the cradle. Damn, he'd wanted Dominiqua to give him a name. At least, however, he had been given a lead. Dominiqua *did* know something. It might take time, but he was certain she would eventually come clean and let him know who had shot down her boyfriend in cold blood.

Nigel shook his head as he thought of last night's murder of a young male. Twenty years old, gunned down in the street. The distraught mother being held up by family members at the crime scene, where her son lay bleeding from a gunshot wound.

Murder on the streets of Cleveland and another young life lost in a senseless manner. When would people stop taking the drastic action of murder as a way to solve their disputes?

Not any time soon, Nigel knew. Ever since his move to the homicide department within the Cleveland police three years earlier, his caseload had always been full.

Marshall Jennings, his best friend of twelve years and partner on the police force, had gone out to speak to the boy's mother once their evening shift had started, while Nigel had stayed in the office looking up information on the victim, that could possibly link to any suspects.

"Hey, Williams."

Nigel, who had been staring at the computer screen, looked to his right. Marshall was heading toward him, his blazer wet. Clearly, he had been caught in the torrential downpour. It was the end of May, and the showers had been intense lately. Mostly because even though it wasn't yet summer, the weather was extremely hot.

The good thing was that if the rain kept up this evening, it wasn't likely anyone would be gunned down on the streets.

"How did it go with the mother and the family?" Nigel asked.

"They're devastated, understandably," Marshall said, shrugging out of his jacket. "They saw Garrett at least two hours before he was shot but don't seem to know anything useful." Marshall hung his blazer on the back of his swivel chair. "They gave me some names of people who might have had a beef with him. Some leads to follow."

"Well, I heard from Dominiqua, the victim's girlfriend," Nigel told him. "Those early leads were right—she *did* see the shooting."

Marshall's eyebrows rose as he took the seat at the desk beside Nigel. "All right. She name the shooter?"

Nigel shook his head. "I tried to get her to come talk to me, or to tell me something over the phone, but she hung up before she did. She's too scared to talk."

Marshall nodded his understanding. "She'll probably come around."

"I hope so. If she loved the guy, I'm thinking she's going to want to see the shooter brought to justice."

"No doubt," Marshall agreed. Leaning forward, he typed

something on his computer screen. Then he said, "Guess who I saw today?"

"Who?"

"Callie."

Callie Hart…Nigel felt as though someone had just punched him in the gut with a sledgehammer. "You did?"

"Yep. I dropped by the church earlier to pay my respects on my way to the dentist. As I was leaving, I saw her getting out of an airport limo."

Nigel turned his attention to the pile of papers on his desk. He needed something to do, a distraction. "So you didn't talk to her?"

"Nope. But get this—she's got a child."

At the news, Nigel whipped his head in his friend's direction. "What?"

"A young boy was getting out of the car with her. Maybe eight. It must be her kid."

Nigel felt a tightening in his chest. Callie had a child? "Was she with someone?" he found himself asking. "A husband?"

Marshall's eyebrows rose at the question. "Still carrying a torch for her, hmm? Even after how she left you?"

"Just curious," Nigel responded. "She's got a kid, she likely has a husband."

"I didn't see her with anyone. It was just her and the kid. But that doesn't mean she's not married. Her husband could have stayed home while she came here for the funeral."

Nigel nodded. He hated that he felt even mildly curious to know what she was doing in her life. Once she had walked away from him, he had vowed to forget her forever.

Obviously, she had forgotten him. If it was true that she had a son around the age of eight, then she had clearly moved on from him fairly quickly. Merely a year or so after breaking his heart, she had gotten involved with someone else and created a child with him.

Well, good for her.

"Another thing," Marshall began, "she looked like she'd been hurt. Was wearing a sling, had a bandage on her forehead. I guess she may have fallen or something."

"Hmm," was Nigel's reply, a noncommittal response. But curiosity was stirring in his gut, even though he didn't want it to.

"You gonna call her up?" Marshall asked.

"Call her?" Nigel guffawed. "Why?"

"To say hi. It's been what, ten years?"

But the look on Marshall's face made it clear that he was simply stirring up trouble. Nigel wondered why his best friend was goading him like this. Marshall knew how brokenhearted he had been after Callie had left town without so much as a glance backward. The last thing Nigel wanted to do now was see her, even if he was over her.

He had already paid his respects to Dave Henry and other family regarding Jean's passing. Thankfully, he hadn't run into Callie at the time.

"Back to the murder case at hand, my friend," Nigel said, turning to his computer. "Because we've got a job to do."

Callie awoke with a start, her eyes popping open. She was surprised to see daylight pouring into the room. It seemed as if she had only gone to bed a short while before, and that the night had whizzed by.

And though she'd clearly slept like a log, she didn't feel well rested. Her mind had been on Nigel before she'd fallen asleep, she had even dreamed of him.

She was anxious, the plight before her weighing on her mind.

Easing her body across the bed, she reached for her phone on the night table with her good arm and checked the time. It was six fifty-two in the morning.

Then she glanced across the room to where the daybed was. Kwame, who had also been exhausted from an early start and hours of activity yesterday, lay on his stomach, his form still. He was sleeping, which didn't surprise Callie.

Quietly, she rose from the bed and exited the room. It was quiet. Perhaps no one had woken up yet.

After using the bathroom, Callie made her way downstairs. As she neared the kitchen, she finally heard soft voices. And when she rounded the corner, she saw Natalie and Uncle Dave sitting at the small, round table.

"Morning," Callie said, then yawned. She wrapped an arm around her uncle, gave him a warm hug. Then she did the same to Natalie.

"I made tea," Natalie said. "But if you want coffee, I can brew a pot."

"I can do it," Callie said.

Natalie stood. "With one good arm? Sit. Let me get you some coffee."

Callie didn't argue. She sat at the table beside Uncle Dave. "How are you feeling today?" she asked him.

"I keep expecting Jean to walk into this kitchen and start fussing about what she's going to prepare." Uncle Dave sighed. "I'm just trying to hang in there."

Reaching across the table, Callie squeezed his hand. There were no words. She could only provide comfort.

Callie turned toward Natalie, who had spent much of the day before inconsolable. "How are you doing today?"

"Better. Definitely better."

Natalie didn't face her as she filled the coffee carafe with water from the sink, and Callie knew this wasn't a good time to ask her about her husband. There would be time for that later.

"Hey, you remember Marshall, Nigel's friend?" Natalie asked as she began to pour the water into the coffeemaker.

"Yeah," Callie said. "Sure I do."

"I saw him yesterday at the church."

"Marshall was at the church?"

"Yeah. You must have just missed him, because I ran into him when I was heading down to the basement to use the bathroom. There he was, exiting the men's room, what a surprise. He'd come to pay his respects, of course, which was nice, though he said he didn't have much time because he was heading to an appointment. He knew Auntie Jean from her volunteer work in the community." Natalie paused. "He mentioned Nigel. Said both of them are detectives now."

Callie felt a spasm of alarm. If Marshall had been at the church, and at the time that Natalie said, then he could have very well seen her. And if he had seen her, he would've seen her with Kwame. Wasn't it likely that he would tell Nigel about having seen her with a young boy?

"Uncle Dave, do you know if Nigel's family still lives at the same house where he did before?" They would be able to tell her how to find Nigel.

"Actually, Nigel lives there now," her uncle answered. "Ever since his father moved south, Nigel's been back there. He spent a lot of time renovating his parents' old house. I hear it's lovely."

If Nigel lived in his parents' old house, that meant he was only two blocks away.

"Good." Callie emitted a shaky breath. "I need to see him."

"Need to see who?"

At the sound of the voice, Callie looked toward the entrance to the kitchen and saw Deanna entering. She was wearing black silk pajamas and a pair of white slippers.

"Nigel," Callie said, then swallowed. "I need to see Nigel."

"Why?" Deanna asked.

"Because I…I need to have an important conversation with

him and I need to have it before anyone else does." Though it could already be too late.

Both of her sisters looked at her with concern. Callie knew they were curious, but she was suddenly anxious. She had to speak to Nigel before Marshall mentioned anything to him. Not that Nigel would necessarily put two and two together, but Natalie's news was a sign that Callie needed to get on with this sooner rather than later.

"Callie?" Natalie prompted in a cautious tone.

Callie knew that what she was about to say would be a bombshell. She hadn't trusted her sisters with the truth at the time because all they'd been doing then was arguing with each other. Somehow, she had come to believe that there'd be no harm in keeping the secret from them.

Same as she'd kept it from Nigel.

That was going to be the hardest part. Doing the right thing and telling Nigel the truth, after all this time.

Callie's stomach twisted. She had loved him. Lord, how she had loved him. But she'd let a disagreement—albeit a major one—come between them.

She held no illusions that she and Nigel would reconnect romantically. Too much time had passed for that to happen. She had gone on with her life, and he had gone on with his. But what she hoped most of all was that he wouldn't be too angry with her when she let him know the truth she had kept from him all these years.

"Whatever it is, Callie," Natalie began gently, "you know that you can trust us with it."

Perhaps Callie should have trusted her sisters with this years ago, but she'd just been so scared. "I have something to tell you," she said, nerves tickling her stomach as she spoke. "Something that I told no one all these years. Except for Tamara Jackson, the friend from college who I went to Florida with. And please, try to understand my reasoning and not be upset with me."

"You're scaring me," Deanna said.

"It's Kwame." Callie looked around, making sure that her son was nowhere in earshot. He had been sleeping when she had left the bedroom, but he could have awoken by now and been on his way downstairs.

Certain that he wasn't lurking nearby, she continued. "When I left Cleveland, I was pregnant. I know you all knew I had a child, and you didn't ask me any questions. Still, I felt the need to tell you that Kwame wasn't Nigel's son. I said nothing more, and I think you all realized that I didn't want to talk about it because you asked me nothing else. Perhaps you even assumed the worst. That I'd broken up with Nigel and met some other guy, quickly got pregnant, and then run. But the truth is..." Callie drew in a deep breath. This was the first stage of her telling the truth. Coming clean. "I was pregnant with Nigel's baby when I left."

"What?" Natalie's eyes bulged. Deanna looked dumbfounded. Uncle Dave, however, didn't look that surprised.

"I was pregnant with Nigel's baby. Things weren't working out, so...I just got scared, thought it would be best to raise the baby on my own."

"I can't believe it," Deanna said. "And I can't believe Nigel let you walk away when you were pregnant with his child."

"No," Callie said, realizing she hadn't been clear. "Nigel had no idea."

"You never told him?" Natalie asked.

"I...I thought it was best."

Deanna was shaking her head. "So now you have to tell him that he's a father?"

"It's going to be hard, but I have to do it. It's the right thing. My accident made that clear. If I were to die, Kwame should know who his real father is." Callie shrugged. "He should have known all along."

Silence fell between them, and after a long moment, Uncle Dave said, "Your aunt figured as much."

Now it was Callie's turn to be surprised. "She—she did?"

"You left town so quickly, then let us know you were pregnant. And the fact that you never wanted to come back to Cleveland… Your aunt realized Nigel must've been the father. I'm sad to say the times we ran into him, we weren't all that friendly. We figured he had done something really bad to hurt you. We blamed him for you not coming back here."

Even more reason for Callie to come clean now. "Nigel and I had our problems, but the decision to leave—that was mine. I was young, scared, and I thought it was the right thing to do. I'm sorry you and Auntie Jean blamed him, because the truth is he didn't do anything particularly horrible to me. We just…I just thought it wasn't going to work between us…" Callie sighed. "Are you all mad at me?"

"No," Natalie said, who moved toward her and hugged her. "I can't say I'll ever truly understand, but this is your business. The only person who has the right to be mad is Nigel."

Callie drew in a deep breath and let it out in a rush. She knew that was true. And that was her biggest fear.

"That's why I have to talk to him. Right now."

"Right now?" Deanna asked. "It's not even seven-thirty in the morning."

"I know, but…" Callie swallowed. "There's no time like the present, right? I've just got to do this, before I lose my nerve."

"At least have some coffee," Natalie told her. She went to the cupboard, got a mug and filled it with java for her sister.

Callie was going to say no, because her stomach was jumpy and she didn't know if she could handle eating or drinking anything. But she was tired, and a jolt of caffeine might do her some good. So she went to the counter, added sugar and cream to her coffee, and took a sip to make sure it was just right.

"Do you want one of us to go with you?" Deanna asked.

Callie waved off the suggestion. "No, definitely not. This is something I need to do on my own."

And it was. She had gotten herself into this mess, and she was the only one who could get herself out of it.

Chapter 3

Nigel Williams could count on one hand the number of times in his life that he'd been speechless. He wasn't the type to find himself at a loss for words. But when he opened the door to his home and saw who stood there—a few minutes shy of eight in the morning—he couldn't think of one thing to say.

He stared, and so did she. He couldn't help wondering if his mind had conjured her, it had been that long.

"Hello, Nigel," came the soft voice of the woman Nigel had once loved. He still didn't speak. He could hardly think, much less form words.

"I know you're surprised to see me," she went on.

Callie Hart was standing on his doorstep. Surprised was an understatement.

Callie looked into Nigel's eyes, then glanced away uncomfortably. His own gaze went to the big white bandage on her forehead. Then he looked lower, noticing that she was hunched into a light jacket that was thrown over her shoulders, as though to protect herself from the chill that had come after the rain. The late May weather had been odd lately, and the recent heat—which had caused the rain—had been followed by a cold spell this morning.

Meeting his gaze once again, Callie asked, "Can I come in?"

Nigel's stomach clenched. Here she was, after not being in touch for ten years, and she was asking to come in as if the request was completely normal? He didn't want to let her in. Not in the least.

"Please," Callie repeated, her voice catching slightly. "It's…it's important."

What could be so important to talk about now, ten years after she had left him?

"Did you walk here?" he asked, looking behind her and seeing no car.

"Yes."

Nigel wanted to turn her away. He really did. No explanation for her behavior would matter at this point.

"Can we please speak inside?" Callie asked. "Because you need to hear me out. Once you do, you can send me away and I'll never return, if that's what you want."

His heart pounding, Nigel contemplated what to do for a moment. Then, he stood back and held the door open wide. As Callie stepped over the threshold, he noticed the sling Marshall had mentioned, which explained why she was wearing the jacket over her shoulders. Marshall had suggested that maybe Callie had fallen, but these injuries looked more serious than that.

"What happened?" Nigel asked, indicating her injury with a jerk of his head.

"A fender bender. Nothing serious."

"You…you seem cold," Nigel found himself saying. "Would you like some tea?"

"That sounds great. Whatever you have."

Nigel closed the front door, then made his way off to the right where the kitchen was. Old habits died hard. He didn't particularly want to offer Callie tea, as if she had come on a social call, but she *was* shivering, and Nigel could hear his mother telling him that you should always offer your guests a drink.

Guest…Callie Hart was hardly a guest.

As he turned on the flame beneath the kettle, he paused at the counter and closed his eyes. And then he pinched himself to make sure that he wasn't dreaming.

He wasn't.

Glancing over his shoulder, Nigel looked at Callie, who was now standing in the living room. She had her good arm wrapped around her body. She was looking around the house with interest, obviously taking in all the changes.

"I hardly recognize the house," she said. "These hardwood floors are beautiful. Are they original?"

"Yeah. Once I ripped up the carpet, I found those floors. I refinished them."

"Beautiful. And I love these upscale light fixtures."

"Thanks," Nigel muttered, wondering why she was talking about the house. "What kind of tea do you want? Orange pekoe, something flavored?"

"Orange pekoe is fine."

Nigel opened the cupboard and took down the box of tea. He got a tea bag and put it into a mug as the water warmed.

"I assume you did all the work?" Callie said.

"Yeah."

"I really like how you opened the place up by knocking down the wall that used to be between the living room and kitchen."

Nigel said nothing. Just gritted his teeth. As if he expected

Callie to be here after all this time, complimenting him on the renovations he'd done to the house.

As the kettle began to boil, Nigel watched Callie move toward the pictures on one of the walls. She seemed to take a keen interest in the photo of him in his police uniform on his graduation day.

"Do you live here alone?" Callie called out.

Nigel didn't answer. Instead, he poured boiling water into the mug. Then, leaving it there to sit, he went back out to the living room.

"Do you live here alone?" Callie repeated.

"If you don't mind, Callie, I'd like you to get to the point of why you're here," Nigel said instead of answering her. "Because I don't understand why, after all this time, you're here at my house."

He saw something flash in her eyes. And he got the distinct sense that all her chatter had simply been a way to break the ice, to ease the tension.

"Maybe you should sit down," she suggested.

Nigel groaned his frustration. "Are you here to apologize, Callie? Because for the life of me, that's the only thing that makes sense. You came back to town for your aunt's funeral, and you've been attacked by a bout of conscience. Well, guess what—you've shown up ten years too late."

"You're angry," she said.

For some reason, the comment irked Nigel all the more. "You're damn right I'm angry." Pausing, Nigel drew in a slow breath. "I mean, I was angry. But what happened was a long time ago."

"I know."

It hurt to see her, he realized. More than it should given how much time had passed. Suddenly, he didn't care if she had that cup of tea. He was ready for the visit to be over.

"You know what, Callie—there's no need to apologize."

If she was truly sorry, it wouldn't have taken her ten years to show up at his door, so any apology she gave him now would ring hollow.

"I'm not here to apologize."

That got his attention. One of his eyebrows shot up. "Then why are you here?"

"Because I need to tell you something. Something I should have told you a long time ago." Callie drew in a deep breath. "Nigel…when I left Cleveland…" Her voice trailed off.

He studied her, wondering what on earth she had to say. Surely she wasn't going to tell him that she regretted leaving, that she wanted him back.

The idea was laughable. But the fact that she was here meant hell had already frozen over, so anything was possible.

"You're here, Callie," he said. "Just spit out whatever it is that you have to say."

"When I left here, I was pregnant," she began slowly, not looking into Nigel's eyes.

Nigel was confused. "I don't understand."

"When I left Cleveland, I was pregnant," she repeated, her eyes now meeting his.

"What are you saying? That you were seeing someone else? Is that why you left without an explanation?"

"No, I wasn't seeing anyone else." Callie spoke emphatically. "What I'm saying is…I was pregnant with *your* baby." Nigel saw her chest rise and fall with a shaky breath. "Nigel, you have a son."

Seconds passed. Seconds in which it seemed as though a bomb had gone off, shattering his world.

In fact, he was certain that Callie had not said what he thought she'd just said. It didn't make sense. If she had been pregnant with his baby, surely she wouldn't have taken off without telling him.

"What did you say?" he asked. He needed to be sure.

"I was pregnant, Nigel. I…I had your baby. A boy. He's here with me—"

"You're telling me I'm a *father*?"

Callie nodded. "Yes. Your son's name is Kwame."

The simple words hit Nigel with the impact of a kick to his stomach, so much so that he exhaled all the air in his lungs in a huge gush.

"I have a…" *Son*? He couldn't even say the word, it was that unbelievable.

"I know you're surprised," Callie went on.

"Surprised?" Nigel laughed, but it was a hollow, mirthless sound. Surprise was the least of it. He was dumbfounded. If someone had told him that his best friend was actually a robot, he would have been less surprised.

He was a father.

It seemed inconceivable. Sure, he knew that he and Callie had made love enough times to create a baby. But though they'd been young, they'd been smart enough to use protection.

"How?" Nigel asked. "How is this possible?"

"I know it's hard to believe because we were using protection," Callie began. "But condoms aren't always foolproof."

This couldn't be happening. Surely Nigel had been transported to the twilight zone. Because what he was hearing was too bizarre to be true.

Get this—she's got a child. Marshall's words sounded in his mind. *A young boy was getting out of the car with her. Maybe eight.*

"How old is he?" Nigel asked.

"Nine."

Nine… If the kid was nine, it certainly could be his son. His heart was racing, but with each passing second, he was becoming convinced that he wasn't in the twilight zone.

This was really happening. This was true.

Callie had said that condoms weren't always foolproof, and Nigel couldn't help remembering at least a couple times that the condom had broken when they'd been together. At the time, he hadn't been overly concerned about it. Because he had planned to spend his life with Callie, so if they'd created a child together, Nigel would have been fine with that, even if a baby had come along sooner than he had planned.

Callie, the condom broke, Nigel remembered telling her the first time it had happened.

Do you think we made a baby? Callie had asked, stroking his face, smiling as if the idea pleased her.

Nigel stiffened his jaw now, pushing the memory of that happier time from his mind. Clearly, he and Callie *had* created a baby one of the times that the condom had broken.

Kwame. His son.

"So you got pregnant and you didn't tell me," Nigel said, stating the obvious.

"I know I should have."

"Yet you didn't."

"Yes," Callie said, sounding ashamed.

It didn't make sense that she was here. Why tell him about this now?

"So what happened to bring you here now? You had some sudden epiphany that you should finally clue me in?"

"Something like that."

He supposed what he really wanted to know was if Callie had ever planned to tell him. "Was that your plan all along?" he asked. "To not tell me about this?"

"No, that wasn't my plan," Callie explained. "I never thought I would have your baby and not tell you about it."

"Then how could you? After what we meant to each—" The words died in Nigel's throat. Obviously, he hadn't meant as much to Callie as he'd thought.

"I just…I felt that if we weren't working as a couple, then why burden you with a child?"

Nigel gaped at her, then steeled his jaw in anger. "Are you serious?"

Callie looked somewhat hurt by the question, but for goodness' sake, he was the one with the reason to be upset. For ten years, she had kept him in the dark. Starting with her pregnancy and then the birth of their son.

"I know it's not easy to understand," Callie said. "I'm not asking for you to forgive me. I know that would be unrealistic. I'm just asking…I'm here because I know it was time for me to do the right thing."

"Because of what happened to you?" Nigel asked, gesturing to her injured arm. "That bandage and sling have something to do with you wanting to do the right thing? Did you get hurt in some…some crazy protest?" He would bet money on it. Callie, the fireball of passion he had known and loved, ready to speak out against injustice at every turn.

Callie looked away, pausing briefly before answering. "No, no protest. I'm not the same person I was years ago. But yes, getting hurt made me see the light. I realized that if I died, Kwame deserved to be with his father."

"So if not for your accident, you wouldn't be here."

"And Auntie Jean's death as well," Callie said softly. "A death in the family put things into perspective."

Nigel gritted his teeth. He wanted to hear Callie say that after all these years, nagging guilt was why she was finally here at his place. He didn't want to hear that he was the fallback plan. That if something tragic happened to her, he would then be good enough for his son.

"A lot of holes with that plan, I can tell you," Nigel muttered.

"I know it wasn't the best pl—"

"For example, let's just say something happened to you

and suddenly Kwame was transferred to my care without knowing who I was. How damaging do you think that would be? Don't you think it would've been better for me to forge a relationship with him ahead of time, not in case of emergency?" Nigel knew that he sounded angry, but damn it, he had a right to be.

Callie closed her eyes and inhaled deeply. "That's why I'm here now. What happened to me was a huge wake-up call, and thankfully the worst didn't happen. Thankfully, you can now forge that relationship with your son. I'm here, Nigel, ready to do the right thing. But if you don't want to be a part of your son's life—"

"Don't you dare say that to me," Nigel said. "You're the one who took my son away from me. You took away my choice to be a father."

"I'm sorry. I…"

"I know. You were hoping I would give you an excuse." When she met his eyes with a questioning expression, he continued. "Give you an excuse to run again."

Callie said nothing, and Nigel nodded. "I know you too well, don't I?"

"I'm here because I want you to get to know your son."

"How generous of you." Nigel turned, began to pace. He needed to move. He needed to do something to help calm his frayed nerves.

He heard the soft breath that escaped Callie's lips, and hated himself for even feeling a measure of empathy for her. He knew how hard it was for her to be here, admitting the truth. But the bottom line was, *she* was the one who had lied to *him*.

Ten years ago, if she had made a soft little sound like that, he would have curled her into his arms and held her until everything was all right.

But there would be no holding her now.

"I'm sorry," Callie said.

Nigel faced her again. "Yeah, well, that apology is ten years too late."

He began to pace again, and silence fell between them, the only sound in the room their heavy breathing.

When he faced her again, he saw that her eyes were filled with tears. And damn it, there was that empathy again. Empathy that she didn't deserve.

Pausing, Nigel drew in a deep breath, one he hoped would help calm his ire. "Look, you can't show up nine years after our son was born and expect me to jump up and down at your news."

"I didn't say that," Callie said softly. She wiped a tear that had fallen down her cheek. "You think this is only hard for you? Being here is the hardest thing I've ever had to do. In many ways, it would have been easier to keep you in the dark. But I *know* how wrong I was, and that's why I'm here now, realizing that you'll likely hate me forever for what I did. Yes, it took a life-altering event for me to realize exactly what's important in life. And I know that now. My son has a father. It's time he get to know him. What I need to know is if you're willing to get to know Kwame."

"Of course," Nigel quipped. "I have a son. I won't turn my back on him."

Callie nodded. "I know you're angry. I also know that I have to deal with whatever reaction you have to this, because this is completely my fault. But I'm figuring you probably need a day or two to let this all sink in, and then maybe we can set up a time for you to meet Kwame—"

"Today. I want to meet him today."

"Are you sure?"

"Yes," Nigel said. Then he groaned. "Damn it, I completely forgot that I have court this morning. Then I have to work this evening. Today isn't the best day."

"We can set up another time," Callie said softly.

"I've missed nine years of his life. I need to meet my son as soon as possible."

Callie nodded. "Good. Because I'm not sure when I'm heading back to Florida, but it's fair to say that time is of the essence. And I'd like for Kwame to spend as much time getting to know you before we leave."

"When's his birthday?" Nigel asked.

"November twenty-eighth."

Nigel processed the information. That would make Kwame's birth just about six months after Callie had disappeared from his world.

"Does he know about me?" Nigel asked.

Callie didn't look at him as she spoke. "No. Not yet. I wanted to wait to see what you would say before I told him."

"And if I didn't want to see him, you would let him continue to live in the dark? Not know about me?"

"No," Callie said slowly. "If you didn't want to see him, then I would have found a way to explain that to him. But I didn't want to get his hopes up about you and the fact that you lived in Cleveland if you didn't want to see him."

Nigel was silent for a long moment, weighing the validity of her answer. He stared at her, and she held his gaze, not flinching.

"Fair enough," he finally said. "As much as I want to meet him today, it'll have to be tomorrow morning. Around ten? If you're going to spring it on him that I'm his father, he might need a little time to process the information. Maybe it's best that I won't have adequate time until tomorrow."

Callie nodded. "Sure, we can come by at ten."

"Good."

Callie offered him a weak smile. Then she turned toward the door.

"Your tea," Nigel said. "You didn't drink it."

"Um, I'll be fine. It's probably best I get back to the house, talk to Kwame."

She made her way to the front door, and Nigel followed her. His heart was beating a mile a minute, he realized. But how could it not be? His life had just changed, in an instant.

"I'll see you tomorrow then," Callie said as she opened the door. "We both will."

"Sure. Now, are you going to tell me what else is going on?"

Callie's eyes widened. "What are you talking about?"

"Call it a cop instinct," he said.

Callie didn't speak right away, just looked at him with that wide-eyed expression. He'd been a cop for nine years, and over that time had honed his senses. Every sense within him told him that Callie was keeping something from him.

"Besides, I don't believe you came here simply because you had an attack of conscience," he added.

Callie wrung her hands together, a sign that he was right on the money. But she didn't speak.

"Does it have to do with the fact that your arm is in a sling?" Nigel asked. "Because that's what my senses are telling me."

"Your senses are off in this case," Callie said. "My aunt died. Like I said, that's the reason I'm here. It made me realize life is too short."

Nigel shrugged. If that was how she wanted to play this, then fine. Why should he care whatever personal mess she might be in?

What mattered was that he had a son.

A son… The gravity of the situation hit him anew.

The woman he had loved more than any other had not only left him, she'd left him and kept their child a secret.

Nigel had always believed that Callie had loved him, loved him as deeply as he loved her, but it was glaringly clear now that she hadn't loved him that much at all.

Chapter 4

After Callie left Nigel's house, her heart beat furiously the entire walk back to Uncle Dave's place. Her stomach was so upset, she actually felt pain.

Telling Nigel that he was a father had been the hardest thing she had ever done. The look on his face, one of utter devastation, still haunted her. At first, he had been bewildered, but the stunned look on his face had quickly morphed into devastation as he had accepted the truth.

Then had come the anger.

He had a right to be angry, absolutely he did, but Callie couldn't imagine how things would go between them from here on out. Clearly, they would have to spend time together in order for Nigel to get to know Kwame. But if how she felt now was any indication of how awkward she would feel when she brought Kwame around, she wasn't certain she could handle it.

You can, she told herself. *If you can handle Auntie Jean dying, you can handle this. If you could handle your mother disappearing, you can handle this.*

This was just another hard thing in her life that she had to deal with.

Her mind replayed her meeting with Nigel. He hadn't been easy on her, which she understood, but some of his comments were uncalled for. It was clear he was automatically thinking the worst of her, despite the fact that she had come to rectify a wrong. Yes, her actions ten years ago had been despicable, and she supposed he simply couldn't trust that her motives now were altruistic. Too much time had passed for her to expect him to know her anymore.

He did, however, seem to sense that there was something more going on with her, as evidenced by his asking more than once about her injuries. Callie hoped her lie would satisfy him, because she didn't want to get into the real reason of why her arm and head had been hurt. Her friend Tamara's plight wasn't his problem. And the last thing she wanted to appear to be doing was using Tamara's dilemma to gain any sympathy from him.

She supposed she should be happy that he'd let her into the house, allowed her any time to speak.

Her stomach tickled as she recalled the first sight of him after ten years. He still looked good. She had always loved his tall frame, and his six-foot-two body was now packed with more muscles than when she had last seen him.

He had been attractive then, with his easy smile, bright eyes and that chiseled jawline. But good Lord, he was even more handsome now.

Callie frowned as she turned onto the street that would lead back to her childhood home. Was she actually feeling a stirring in her gut? A pull of attraction for the man she had once loved?

It was insane, wasn't it?

And yet when she thought of him again, wearing only an undershirt, and the sight of his strong, hard muscles and that smooth dark skin…

She was insane. Clearly, she was. How could she feel any morsel of a reaction to his looks after all this time?

The answer to that was clear. She may have put time and distance between them, emotionally cutting him off, but her body still reacted to him as a woman.

As Nigel headed toward the courthouse, he couldn't even force himself to think about the murder case where he was about to give testimony. Instead, his mind was on Callie and her bombshell.

There he was at home, getting ready for work as usual, and before he'd left his house he had learned that he was a father.

A father… He had a son.

Nigel was experiencing a whole host of emotions that he couldn't make sense of. He thought he would only feel anger and betrayal, but there were other emotions in the mix.

And of those, the overwhelming emotion was fear.

He was a father.

Tomorrow, he would meet his son for the first time.

This was wrong. A man shouldn't meet his son for the first time at nine years old. He should meet him in the hospital, the moment he is born.

Nigel's hands felt jittery, and he clenched the steering wheel of his unmarked police car to steady them. Had he ever been this anxious? He was scared to meet his child, and that was wrong on so many levels.

Perhaps scared was the wrong word. But he was definitely nervous. Because nine years was a long time for his child to have not known him. What if he didn't like him? What if he rejected him as his father? Those were very real possibilities, all because Callie had selfishly lied. He didn't care if they had broken up at the time. She had to know that he was the kind of man who would have done right by his child, no ifs, ands, or buts.

She'd taken away his right to be a father, and that was unforgivable.

As the downtown courthouse came into view, Nigel drew in a deep breath hoping to calm himself. He was angry, yes. But he knew he had to find a way to move past the angry feelings, because they would not be constructive in this situation.

Because the bottom line was that he was father. In an instant, he had learned that he was responsible for the rearing of a human being.

Callie had planned to go directly to Uncle Dave's house, but instead she kept walking. She strolled the streets of her old neighborhood, marveling at how different it looked. As a teen, the streets had seemed so big and almost intimidating. But as an adult, they were so much smaller.

As she walked, her mind was on the pressing situation at hand. She would have to talk with her son. She would have to explain to him that he had a father, and that he was going to meet him very soon.

All night, Callie had been concerned about Nigel's reaction to her deception. Now, she was worried about her son's reaction. The son she had always told to tell the truth no matter the consequences, would no doubt be hurt to know that she had not been truthful with him.

She could only do what had to be done, and hope that her son understood.

She made her way back to the house, where upon entry, she could see everyone was in the kitchen at the back. Kwame was seated at the table with Natalie and Uncle Dave, while

Deanna was at the stove, tending to a pan of sizzling bacon. Kwame was chuckling about something someone had said.

"Naw, not really," Kwame said.

"I don't believe that," Natalie responded. "I'm certain you're very popular at your school. I know your mother's going to have to watch over you like a hawk. All those girls who'll want to date you…"

Crossing her arms over her chest, Callie entered the kitchen. "Hiya, everyone. Exactly what are you all talking about?"

"We were telling your son how handsome he is," Natalie explained, running a hand over his head.

Deanna, who was at the stove cooking, grinned at her. "And we were finding out the skinny on if he has any girlfriends."

"Girlfriends?" Callie asked, surprised. "He's nine."

"Times have changed," Uncle Dave said.

"That's for sure," Natalie agreed. "Love blooms younger than that these days. I have friends who tell me that their five- and six-year-olds are talking about who their girlfriends and boyfriends are in their classrooms. Obviously it's all very innocent at that age, but still."

"I'm certain my son has no girlfriends," Callie said. And she was happy to keep it that way, as her son was too young for that nonsense.

But when Kwame actually flashed a nervous look, then glanced downward, Callie couldn't have been more surprised.

Did he have a girlfriend? Obviously not a girlfriend in the true sense of the word, but someone that he liked?

She made her way over to him and sat at the table beside him. "Son? You—you have a girlfriend?"

"Well, I do kind of like this one girl in my class. Felicity."

"Felicity?" Callie repeated, stunned. Her son had never mentioned this to her.

Kwame shrugged. "Kind of. A little."

Callie knew that he and Felicity liked to study together, and she was one of the girls in the neighborhood who lived close enough that they could hang out sometimes. But to learn that her son actually had a crush on her...

Well, she supposed everyone had their secrets.

"Help yourself to coffee," Deanna said. "We waited until Kwame woke up to start breakfast, so your timing is good. The scrambled eggs and bacon are almost done. And there are fresh biscuits in the oven."

The kind of breakfast Auntie Jean used to make on a week-end morning. Callie's stomach growled but, although she was hungry, she knew she was too anxious to eat. "I'll just have some of that coffee for now."

"You're not eating?" Natalie asked.

Callie shook her head. "Not yet."

Natalie held her gaze for a beat, then nodded. She was clearly curious as to how the meeting with Nigel went, but she knew she would have to wait to ask.

Callie went over to the coffeepot and poured herself a tall mug. She hadn't had the tea at Nigel's place, and she needed this.

"It really is nice to have you all here," Uncle Dave said. "You're filling this house with warmth, now that your Auntie Jean's gone."

Taking a seat between Uncle Dave and Kwame, Callie patted her uncle's hand. Not for the first time, she thought about how she had always hoped to marry a man who loved her as much as Uncle Dave had loved her aunt.

"It does me good, having you here with me," he said. "It's been too long."

"I know," Callie said softly. "I know."

She was going to tell Kwame that they needed to talk, but no one had eaten yet, so Callie decided to wait until he'd finished his breakfast. She had a second cup of coffee, but nothing else. She couldn't eat when she was anxious.

There was more laughter during the breakfast conversation, but at one point there were also tears. Each day, Auntie Jean's passing would get a little easier to bear, but she knew there were still many tears to come.

After Kwame was finished, Callie pushed her chair back and stood. She placed her hand on his shoulder and said, "Son, we need to have a talk."

Kwame looked up at her and concern. "Is everything okay?"

Given that she hadn't eaten, Callie knew he would be concerned. She preached the value of eating a good breakfast. "Yes," she told him, patting his shoulder. "I'm fine. It's just…I need to have a private talk with you about something."

Kwame looked at her with curious eyes. "Did I do something wrong?"

"No, son. You didn't do anything wrong. We just need to talk, that's all."

As she left the kitchen, Callie looked over her shoulder. Deanna gazed at her and nodded, silently giving her encouragement.

Though Deanna and Natalie had spoken in general at breakfast, Callie noted that they hadn't truly spoken to each other. There was clearly still awkwardness, which she supposed was to be expected, given the rift that had been between them.

But that was an issue Callie would have to worry about later. For now, she had to deal with breaking the news to her son that he had a father.

Walking with him upstairs, she led him to the bedroom, then sat him on the bed. She took a seat beside him and covered his hands with hers.

"What is it, Mom?" Kwame asked, his eyes wide with concern.

"I have something important to tell you." She sighed. "And it's not easy for me. But I want you to know that whatever questions you have, I'll answer. Okay?"

Kwame nodded. "Okay."

Callie paused a moment, gathering her courage, then forged ahead. "Remember how when you asked me who your father was, and I told you he was someone from my past? That I had my reasons for leaving him and didn't want to say much more?"

Kwame nodded. "Yeah."

Callie had known that her son had more questions, but he had respected her. He was sensitive that way. She guessed that he assumed she would tell him more when she was ready.

"Well, I want to tell you about your father now. He lives here, in Cleveland."

She watched as his eyes grew as wide as saucers. "He does?"

"Yeah."

A long beat passed. Then Kwame softly said, "I always thought my dad was dead."

"You did?"

"Uh-huh. I thought…I thought if he was alive, you would have told me about him."

Callie smiled softly. Of course. In his young mind, he had come up with a reasonable explanation for his father's absence in his life. Because Kwame knew other kids whose parents weren't together, but they still had a relationship with both their mother and father. He had clearly figured his father was dead for him not to know him at all.

The fact that Kwame had assumed his father was deceased made Callie feel even worse for her having kept him in the dark all these years.

"He's definitely not dead," Callie said. "And what I'm going to say may be hard for you to hear. I only hope that you know that it wasn't my intention to hurt you."

Kwame nodded.

"Your father and I…before you were born, we'd had our differences. Differences that led me to believe that raising you alone was the best thing. I didn't even tell him I was pregnant." Callie paused, noted that her son was looking at her with interest and compassion, not judgment. He was wise beyond his years.

"It was the wrong decision, honey. And a big part of me feels embarrassed to admit this to you, but I don't want you to be mad at him."

"So he never knew about me?" Kwame asked. "At all?"

"No, sweetheart. I want to make that clear to you. It's not like your father knew you existed and chose not to be a part of your life. I…I feel awful for what I did, but all I can say is that at the time, I had my reasons. Reasons that seemed good to me. A lot has happened in the last couple weeks that has made it clear that I was wrong, and that you ought to know who your father is." Callie paused. "So that's where I went this morning. To see your father and tell him about you."

Kwame was silent, and Callie could see in his eyes that he was processing everything. After several seconds, he asked, "What did he say?"

"That he wants to meet you."

Kwame's smile was hesitant. "He did?"

"Of course." She ran a hand over his head affectionately. "Of course he would." She kissed Kwame's cheek. "I'm sorry I didn't tell you about him before, but I was scared."

"You were?"

"Yes. With each day that passed that I didn't tell you about your father and where he lived, it became harder to know what to say to you when the time came. Mostly because I wasn't ready to contact him about you. I was worried about how he would react if I told him the truth."

"Was he mad?"

Callie nodded. "Uh-huh," she said, opting for the truth. "But he had a right to be. And he could have been more upset. But the most important thing for him was learning that he had a son."

Another pause ensued. Then Kwame asked, "What's his name?"

"His name is Nigel. Nigel Williams."

"What does he do?"

"He's a police officer. Actually, a detective. He solves murders."

"Cool," Kwame said.

Callie was glad that her son was immediately warming to the idea of having a father, rather than being shocked and hurt that she hadn't told him the truth all along.

But he didn't say what she had expected him to say, that he wanted to meet his father, so Callie asked. "Honey, do you want to meet him? I know this is all so sudden—"

"I want to meet him today," Kwame said with enthusiasm. Then he immediately glanced away. "Unless…unless you don't want me to."

Callie's heart ached to hear those words from her son's mouth, but could she blame him? "The whole reason I'm telling you about him is because I want you to get to know him," she explained. "I figured that you might need some time before meeting him, to process it all, but it seems that you're as eager to meet him as he is to meet you."

"Will it be today?" Kwame expelled an audible breath, one full of nervousness.

"As I said, your father is a police officer, so he's got to go to court today and work later, but tomorrow morning, we'll go meet him. Sound good?"

"Sure," Kwame said.

"Great." Now Callie was the one to exhale nervously. This was really going to happen. Kwame and Nigel would finally meet.

"Can I go downstairs now?" Kwame asked.

"Of course."

As he bounded out of the room, a smile touched Callie's lips. Her son had taken this news very well.

Thank God for the resilience of children.

But the real test would come tomorrow.

Chapter 5

Nigel had planned not to tell Marshall about Callie's revelation until after he met his son. But it didn't take long after
they started their evening shift for Marshall to realize that he
was completely distracted and ask him what was going on.

So he told him. Told him about the surprise visit from
Callie and what she'd said.

Marshall stared at him with the same dumbfounded expression Nigel was sure he'd worn this morning when Callie
had stunned him with her news.

"What?" Marshall asked. "What did you just say?"

Nigel expelled a huff of air. He'd spent the day trying to
get a handle on his emotions. He kept alternating between
being confused, surprised and angry.

Right now, after having relayed the story to Marshall, he
was back to being livid. "She said that I'm a father."

"No way."

"That's what she says."

"So the kid she was with… About eight, right?"

"He's nine," Nigel said. "The timing fits. The date of his birth is six months after we broke up."

"I can't believe it, man. What are you going to do?"

"It's all just sinking in," Nigel told him. "The reality of it. I didn't wake up expecting to learn that I'm a father. The situation is so surreal. But that said, if the kid is mine—"

Nigel didn't finish what he was saying. A part of him never wanted to see Callie again, not after her revelation. He had loved her, but clearly she hadn't loved him at all. For her to leave him, while carrying his child, and wait ten years to tell him about this… If that wasn't the lowest of the low, then what was?

"You believe her?"

"Yeah, I do." And that was the problem. Because considering he believed her, then he had no choice but to get to know his child. Which meant he had to see Callie again, even if that was the last thing he wanted to do.

"I wish I could throw her in jail for this," Nigel went on. "Lock her up and throw away the key." But even as he said the words, he knew he was lying. He was speaking the language of an angry man. One who had been deceived. "But if Kwame is my son…" He paused, once again feeling the gravity of the situation.

He was a father.

"Then you're gonna accept him," Marshall supplied.

"Yeah."

"Of course. I knew that for you there would be no other choice. You're not the type to turn your back on your child, even under these circumstances." Marshall paused, his eyes widening as he shook his head. "But it's gonna be hard, man. To not have been in the kid's life all this time… He might reject you."

Marshall knew him too well. He'd been a friend of Nigel's

for twelve years, ever since they'd met at college. They'd both gone on to become police officers, following a similar path within the police force. Nigel had become a sergeant in six years, Marshall in seven. Nigel became a detective three years ago, and Marshall followed him a year later. The best friends were now partners.

So Marshall knew there was no way that Nigel could walk away from his son, whether or not he'd known he existed. Nigel was the kind of man who, if he had fathered a child during a one-night stand, would've been in the child's life as a full-time father.

This child, however, had been born out of love.

Love, he thought sourly. He had loved Callie, but how did a woman who had claimed to love him lie to him for all these years?

"No matter how hard it will be, I have to be in his life," Nigel said. "Take it slow. Day by day."

"I hear that," Marshall said. He got up from his desk, picking up Nigel's coffee mug as he did. "I'm thinking you need another one, right?"

Again, proof that his friend knew him too well. The more stressed Nigel was, the more coffee he drank. It was like that when they worked a murder case together. He could drink a whole pot of coffee in one shift. For him, it had the effect of calming his nerves, as opposed to making him more on edge.

"Yeah, sure," Nigel told him.

As his friend went off to get the coffee, Nigel thought again about seeing Callie on his doorstep. To think that for one fleeting moment he had fantasized—as his eyes had first settled on her in surprise—that she'd shown up at his door to tell him that she still loved him. That she regretted walking out on him and wanted him back in her life.

How foolish had he been.

Ten years, and clearly he was still delusional regarding Callie Hart.

There was a time when Nigel had believed that he was going to marry Callie, that they would settle down and have the family he had always dreamed of having with her. But after she had walked away from him with not so much as a goodbye, he had become jaded and distrustful. Ultimately, he had started dating again, but he hadn't felt for anyone else what he had felt for Callie.

At his house, she had asked him if he was involved with anyone, and he had avoided her question. He was single now, though a couple years ago he had gotten engaged with the hope of finally having that family he craved. The truth was, Angie had been more of a good friend with potential than a woman he loved. And she knew it too, because even though she'd said yes to his proposal, she had ultimately given him a myriad of excuses as to why they shouldn't get married— she was afraid of being a cop's wife, he didn't spend enough time with her, that sort of thing. If Nigel had loved her the way he should have, he would have fought to keep her in his life, but instead he had let her walk away.

Unlike some of the guys he knew—like Marshall, who preferred to date but not settle down—Nigel was the marrying kind. He relished the idea of settling down and having a family. Most likely because although his parents had been married for thirty-seven years before his mother's death, they had hardly been in love. His father had never looked at his mother with genuine affection. He always got the sense that the two of them had just been friends who one day said, *Why don't we tie the knot?*

Perhaps in their generation that was the thing to do. Or perhaps something happened during the marriage that Nigel didn't know about that caused a rift between them. Regardless, Nigel had craved a close relationship with a woman and a house full of kids.

Stupid fool that he was, even as he and Angie had broken up, he had thought of Callie. Wondered where she was and what she was doing with her life.

It wasn't that he couldn't track her down. He was a cop, with the resources to find her. He simply hadn't wanted to. He hadn't wanted to know what was going on in her life. He hadn't wanted to think of her. He had wanted to close his heart to her once and for all.

Marshall reappeared with a cup of black coffee just as Nigel liked it.

"My, my, my, Callie is back in town," Marshall mused. "You know, I always thought you two were perfect for each other. Shocked me big time when she left. I guess if that friend of hers had never been so brutally beaten, then she wouldn't have been so angry with you when you—"

"Then it would've been something else," Nigel said, spitting out the words. "She took the first excuse and ran with it. If it wasn't what happened to her friend, then she would have found another excuse."

Nigel shrugged, as though what he'd just said was hardly of consequence to him, but the truth was, just thinking of what Callie had done was making his gut clench painfully right now.

Which was crazy. Because he shouldn't feel anything. Nothing at all.

Callie had thought she was nervous heading to see Nigel yesterday and telling Kwame the truth about his father, but now, as she woke up on the day they would all meet, her nerves were even more shot.

She had hardly slept all night, so consumed with the thoughts of how the meeting would go. Callie had noticed that even Kwame tossed and turned as he slept. He had taken the news with stride yesterday, but it was clear that her son was anxious over the idea of meeting his father. He was only nine years old, and despite being mature for his age, he was still a kid.

A kid who was no doubt worried about whether or not his father would accept him.

Callie hoped that the visit went well. She wished she could predict how both Kwame and Nigel would react to each other, but that would only be revealed with time.

Callie saw to it that Kwame had a good breakfast, one where the family was once again gathered. Everyone except Deanna. She had left yesterday afternoon to visit a friend and hadn't returned. Despite what Deanna had said about being willing to put the past with Natalie behind them, Callie doubted they had straightened things out.

But she would have to worry about that later. Right now, she had to introduce her son to his father.

Precisely at 10:00 a.m., Callie was at Nigel's door with Kwame. She knocked, and then held her breath as she waited for Nigel to answer.

Moments later the door opened, and there was Nigel. He held her gaze for one electrically charged moment, and the air in Callie's lungs expelled in a rush. She felt a tingling of what she'd felt yesterday—a definite reaction to him as a man.

Even after all this time, her body reacted to his. She supposed she shouldn't be surprised. Their physical connection had always been intense.

The next moment, Nigel's gaze went from her to Kwame. He said nothing, just stared, taking in the sight of him.

Callie saw a wealth of emotions flash in his eyes. Wonder, fear, excitement, sadness. In twenty-four hours, Nigel's life had changed forever.

Callie cleared her throat and looked from Nigel to her son. "Kwame," she said, "this is your father."

Then Callie regarded her son cautiously. His eyes were wide as he looked at Nigel. He was clearly curious, but also overwhelmed.

And then she noticed Kwame swallow, and she saw in that simple motion his vulnerability. He was standing here on his father's doorstep, looking for acceptance. For some sign that his biological father was not going to reject him.

Her gaze volleyed back to Nigel. The fear was gone, and Callie saw in his eyes hope, caution and vulnerability, same as the look on Kwame's face. They were both looking for acceptance.

Nigel was the one to make the first move. He extended a hand to Kwame, saying, "Hello."

"Hi," Kwame said in a meek voice.

Nigel opened the door wide. "Both of you come on in."

Kwame stepped forward first, followed by Callie. When they were in the foyer, Kwame asked, "Are you my dad? Is it really true?"

Nigel got down on his haunches so that he was eye level with his son. "Yeah. And I want you to know that I just found out about you and I couldn't be happier." Nigel smiled, a genuine smile that reached his eyes. "I wish I had known about you before, but I'm meeting you now. And that's what matters."

Kwame nodded.

Nigel continued to speak. "I'm sure you probably have questions for your mother, and the two of you likely already discussed the situation. But I just wanted to say to you that if you're angry with her for anything, don't be. Your mother and I…our relationship was difficult at times but it had nothing to do with you. I know she didn't want to hurt you. So I just want to make sure that you're not angry with her."

Callie's eyes immediately went to Nigel's, and he met her gaze. She was certain she had a look of wonder on her face, because she was shocked. Shocked and touched at the fact that he was trying to make sure her son absolved her of any guilt. It was far more generous of him than he needed to be.

Nigel suddenly said, "Oh, heck. Forget all this formality. I want to give you a hug." He drew Kwame into a warm hug, one that lasted for several seconds. Nigel hugged his son, and Kwame hugged him back. Callie's eyes filled with tears. Kwame's eyes were shut tight as he held his dad, but there was a big smile on his face, one she knew meant total bliss.

She had just given her son the father he'd always wanted.

Chapter 6

Nigel and Kwame spent the next few hours talking and getting to know each other. The talking portion didn't last very long, because once Nigel asked Kwame if he liked to play basketball, and Kwame said that he did, Nigel suggested they head out to the driveway and shoot some hoops. Nigel had a basketball net set up over the garage door, something that hadn't been there when Callie had been dating him. Nigel got her a folding chair from in the garage, and she sat and watched as her son and her former lover bonded over basketball.

They took turns shooting the ball into—and at—the hoop. Kwame's laughter was easy, his bonding with his father well underway. Callie had no doubt that there would be challenges to come; she didn't expect everything to be one-hundred-percent perfect and easy. But for now, Nigel and Kwame were making leaps and bounds toward becoming father and son.

Callie smiled as she watched Nigel lift Kwame to the basket so that he was able to dunk the basketball. Releasing him onto the ground a moment later, Kwame turned to give him a high five.

And again that smile. Kwame was happier than Callie had seen him in a long time.

"Mom," Kwame said, turning to face her. "Do you want to try?"

"Oh gosh, no." Callie waved off the suggestion. "I'm not good at basketball." Not that she couldn't try, but this was about Kwame and Nigel. About them bonding. And they were definitely doing that. It was much more than Callie could have hoped for.

As she watched Nigel interacting so easily with her son—*their* son—she found herself wondering what life would have been like had they all been together from the start. Would they be a happy family unit? Would she and Nigel be deeply in love still?

Callie emitted a shuddery breath with the thought. There was no doubt that Nigel was a man she could have loved forever. He'd had such control over her heart that she'd known she had to put physical distance between them in order to try to evict him out of her heart.

Because though they'd had a deeply passionate relationship, Callie had come to doubt if he would love her forever. Her life experience had taught her that just because people were supposed to love you forever didn't mean that they would.

People like her mother.

So to begin to raise a family with Nigel, only for differences to tear them apart…Callie had known she wouldn't be able to deal with that. Emotionally, she wouldn't have been able to handle him breaking her heart.

So she had run before things got worse between them, believing that she had no choice but to keep their child a secret from him. It was the only way she had been able to ensure that Nigel would no longer be a part of her life.

But what if she had stayed? What if they had been able to resolve their differences? What if Nigel had been a part of Kwame's life all along?

Just thinking about her former relationship with Nigel had Callie's stomach fluttering, and she tried to push thoughts of the past out of her mind. She wasn't the type of person who believed in what-ifs and could-have-beens. What had happened was a reality she couldn't change.

She watched Nigel do a little dance with the basketball and get past Kwame, who was trying to block him. Beads of sweat were covering Nigel's skin. His forehead, his arms.

His body beneath the T-shirt.

And God, what a body. She hadn't touched him, held him in ten years, and yet as she looked at him, she noticed the way his loose T-shirt was now clinging to parts of his slick torso.

Nigel was a beautiful specimen of a man.

He always had been. His gorgeous looks and his easy smile, in addition to that incredible body, had led her to being one of the many women who had found him attractive in high school, and had vied for his attention. He was a year older than she, and when she had first seen him playing basketball on the court in high school, she never thought she'd ever have a chance with him.

But as luck would have it, she later got to see and meet him when she joined a students' group called SFA—Students For Action—where students got together to deal with injustice. The injustice ranged from bullying to students being left out by classmates and even to kids who were being mistreated by teachers on occasion.

Nigel's face had drawn Callie in, but she'd fallen for his sense of consciousness. Both of them had been passionate about causes greater than their own. Nigel graduated high school first, and went on to continue to fight against injustice while in college. Callie, joining him at Cleveland State a year later, did the same. They had become involved with citywide organizations, lending their voices to support causes that mattered to them.

One case that had really hit close to home for Callie was about a mother of three who, having left an abusive husband, was going to be evicted from her apartment because she didn't make enough money to support them on one income. Without a home, child services would place her children in foster care. Once Callie heard the story, she knew she needed to get involved. Both she and Nigel were active in petitioning to help this young woman. Petitioning soon led to fundraising. They washed cars and went door-to-door collecting money. One night, as Callie had lain in bed with Nigel, she told him that she wanted to do something even bigger to help this woman. For Callie, the idea of this mother losing her children—a mother who *wanted* her children—was too much to bear. She knew that it was entirely personal for her on a level that had more to do with the fact that she had lost her own mother. But she empathized with the mothers willing to do everything they could to save their children.

So she had suggested to Nigel that perhaps they should organize a five-mile run to help raise funds. Nigel had agreed. They brought the idea to their group at Cleveland State, and the next thing they knew they were taking pledges, planning for the big date and getting a lot of media attention. The media was impressed with the students who cared so much that they were willing to go above and beyond to see that this woman did not have to lose her home or her children.

Callie's gaze went back to Nigel. It was hard to forget just how much they'd had in common back then. How much she had loved him. Two people united against injustice.

Callie got up from the chair and went back into the house. The day had warmed up considerably, and Kwame and Nigel could certainly use a drink.

As Callie walked through the house and into the kitchen, she again took in everything she could. If Nigel had a girl-friend, there was no sign of her in his home.

Callie opened the fridge and found a carton of orange juice. She poured two tall glasses and brought them outside.

As she was making her way down the steps, she stopped midstride, noticing that Nigel had taken off his shirt.

And it wasn't so much his beautiful form that had her catching her breath. It was the scar down the middle of his chest.

Even from her vantage point several feet away, she could see that the scar was serious looking. It started a couple of inches beneath his collarbone and was probably around five inches long.

Nigel, who had the ball, either sensed her or saw her in his peripheral vision, because he paused to look at her.

And then Kwame said, "Come on, Dad!"

Emotion threatened to overwhelm Callie. *Dad.* One word, but it meant so much.

"Your mother has some refreshments," Nigel said, indicating Callie with a jerk of his head.

"One more shot," Kwame said in a pleading tone.

"Have something to drink first," Callie said. She knew her son well enough to know that he didn't care about hydrating when he was having fun.

"Let's take a break, have something to drink and then we can get back to the game," Nigel said while he began to walk toward Callie.

As he did, Callie stared at him. Her eyes took in the long, dark scar that had formed a keloid. The scar was in the area of his heart.

What had happened to him? Something to do with his job? Had he been hurt in the line of duty?

Nigel reached for one of the glasses of orange juice. "Thanks."

"You're welcome," Callie told him. She passed the second glass to her son. Then she said, "You know, don't let him tire you out. He's got the kind of energy that will last for hours on end. If you need a break, feel free to say so."

"I'm okay," Nigel told her.

He didn't quite meet her eyes, which reminded Callie of just how awkward the situation was. She wanted to ask him about his scar, if it had something to do with his work, but she didn't feel she had the right.

Because it was Nigel's decision to join the police force—to cross over to the dark side, as she had seen it then—that had been the start of much of their problems.

Back when she'd been in Cleveland, Callie hadn't trusted the police, and Nigel hadn't trusted them all that much, either. There had been far too many cases of young black males who had been beaten while being arrested, or even shot. Cases of what clearly constituted overzealous police officers arresting black males who had gotten into trouble. Yes, some of these youths were clearly acting out, but there had to be a better way to deal with them.

Then came the day when Callie's college friend was out at the mall with some of his buddies, and a store owner complained about the group being too rowdy and called the police. According to the witnesses there, Jeremiah, Callie's friend, had stood up to the police for what he thought was harassment. The college kids were not out to cause trouble, simply hanging out at the mall to pass the time. Somehow things went horribly wrong and an officer struck Jeremiah, who resisted any attempt at being unlawfully detained. It wasn't the smartest thing to do on Jeremiah's part, but he certainly did not deserve the horrific beating that followed. One that landed him in the hospital.

He'd been beaten so badly that he was in a coma with significant brain damage. Brain damage that the doctor said would result in him never living a normal life again. Callie had cried with the family when Jeremiah's parents made the decision to take him off life support. Four days later him, Jeremiah succumbed to his injuries.

Callie had not only been devastated, she had been livid. Members of her college organization, including Nigel, had protested loudly at city hall. In front of police headquarters. They wanted charges drawn against this officer who clearly went too far. They were united in their anger over the fact that something like this could happen in their community to someone who had never even committed a crime. That a young man had to die because of such injustice.

Then, Nigel had done the unforgivable. He had told her, not more than a month after the tragic incident—when after an investigation, no charges were laid against the cop who had taken Jeremiah's life—that he had submitted an application to the police force.

Callie had felt betrayed. How could Nigel join the very group of people who had attacked Jeremiah? Nothing he had said to explain it had made any sense to her at all. As far as she was concerned, good people had likely joined the police force every day, only to be corrupted when given power. And she had no doubt that Nigel would become just like the others, forced to tow the party line. Because the truth was, even after Jeremiah had been killed, the officers who'd witnessed the attack did not take a stand against the officer who'd overzealously beaten him. They had instead defended the cop.

Nigel had decided to join a group of people whom he would have to lie to cover for, even if he himself didn't become one of the bad ones. And Callie hadn't been able to accept that.

She didn't care that his rationale had been that he was trying to make a difference. And that joining the police force was the way he saw fit to affect change. All she saw was that he was becoming the enemy.

They'd had heated arguments over his decision—and then Nigel had done something she hadn't expected. He'd questioned her as to the true nature of her relationship with Jeremiah.

Are you really that upset because I want to become a cop? he had asked her. *Or was there more to your relationship with Jeremiah? Because I understand being upset about what happened, but to not want me to become a cop—that seems over-the-top.*

You're becoming the enemy! Callie had shot back.

The enemy who killed Jeremiah—yeah, I know. I heard you the first time. Tell me, Callie—was there more going on between you two than you've told me? Were you sleeping with him?

Callie had been too indignant to answer. And too crushed that he would even think that. Especially because at the time, she had just discovered that she was pregnant with his child.

Everything had gone downhill between them lightning fast. But the accusation…Callie remembered thinking at the time that if she'd told Nigel she was pregnant, he might not believe the baby was his.

Looking back on it now, she could see that she was young and had acted immaturely by just leaving. But she had been so angry. Suddenly, she and Nigel were fighting all the time, which had been a stark change to their formerly loving relationship. Callie had begun to fear that she'd made the wrong choice in a partner. If they couldn't agree on the issue of him becoming a cop, how could they ever agree on raising a child?

Her decision to leave had been a knee-jerk reaction. She could see that now. Added to that were her sisters' problems—over a man who couldn't be faithful—which Callie had been forced into the middle of. She had started to feel a huge sense of anxiety, that perhaps trusting anyone with her heart was a foolish thing to do. With the exception of her uncle Dave, she didn't know very many good men in the world. Men who you could trust to love you and cherish you forever.

Callie was never one to buy into romantic ideals. Real life had taught her that bad things happened all the time.

Being pregnant and estranged from Nigel, and her sisters, she had left and gone to Florida to live with her college friend, Tamara, who'd decided to head back to Miami to continue her college studies where she could be closer to her family.

Callie opted to pick up her studies—and her life—in Florida.

Nigel had said he wanted to make a difference in the world, and Callie had wanted to do the same, which was what had led her into the field of counseling. She wanted to be able to guide young kids who might be at risk of heading down the wrong path. What better way to reach out to them than through the school system as a counselor? It hadn't been easy, being a single mother. But Callie had always been a fighter. So she made it happen.

It had been a definite challenge to balance working, motherhood and schooling. Giving birth to Kwame the year before she'd finished her undergraduate degree, it had taken Callie an extra year to get her B.A. Then, through sheer dogged determination, she went on to get her Masters in Social Work.

Callie loved her job. She loved working in the school system and knowing that she was making a difference with kids on the fringe. Kids who were at an impasse. Kids who had perhaps gone through hardships in their lives and like her, did not trust authority. She related as well, because she had been one of them. So they instinctively knew that her experience was real. She wasn't just another adult trying to tell them they needed to do the right thing. She was someone who had lived in their shoes, had gone through her own heartbreak and had come out on the other side. She was a living example that you could have a rough past and still go on to be successful.

She had worried that her own son might take a wrong path, secretly angry that he didn't have a father in his life. It was so hard for boys. Callie understood that they especially needed male mentors.

And while Kwame was mostly a good kid, he'd begun acting out last year, talking back, not listening, seeming to disconnect from her and cling to his friends. And Callie had understood why. Because she'd broken up with Philip, the man he'd come to see as a father figure.

Callie focused on her son and his father. How odd that they were all here now, and Kwame seemed happier than ever.

Nigel was what he'd needed all along.

Because Nigel was fitting into the father role as if he'd been one his entire life.

Chapter 7

Callie had no time to get into how her day had gone when she and Kwame returned home shortly after three o'clock, because Uncle Dave, who had been sitting on his recliner, stood the moment she entered the house. "I'm glad you're back," he said, looking stressed.

"Is something wrong?" Callie asked.

"Hell, yes, something's wrong. Turned into world war three after you left. It's a damn shame, I tell you. Your poor aunt's barely been laid to rest and your sisters can't get along, even now."

Callie groaned. "Where are they?"

"Upstairs. In each of their rooms. Haven't seen either of them for a good hour."

Callie started up the stairs. "I'd better talk to them. Help them work things out."

"Actually, I'd like you and your sisters to come to my room. It's time I have a talk with all of you."

Callie stopped. "Oh, sure." She looked beyond her uncle to Kwame. "I imagine Kwame doesn't need to be there?"

"What I have to say is just for you and your sisters."

"All right. Kwame, this would be a good time to set up your Wii system." Callie had had the foresight to pack it, exactly for a time like this. "Uncle Dave, can he set up his game in the living room?"

"Of course."

Her uncle made his way up the stairs, Callie and Kwame followed behind. Callie saw her uncle heading to Deanna's door as she went into the bedroom with Kwame.

She unpacked the Wii system, and Kwame scooped up the games. The two of them brought the system downstairs.

"You've got it, right?" Callie asked, but she already knew that her son knew how to put it together.

"Uh-huh."

"Okay. I'll be upstairs."

Moments later, she was on the second floor of the home and heading to her uncle's bedroom door, which was open. Inside the room, she first saw Deanna, who was standing by the window, her arms crossed over her chest. Then she saw that Natalie was on opposite side of the large bedroom, her eyes cast downward.

Uncle Dave was on the bed. Once Callie entered and came to a stop in the center of the room, Uncle Dave cast a glance at all three sisters in turn and heaved a weary sigh.

"Look at you three," he said. "Unable to get along after all this time. Hell, Deanna, you're standing with your arms crossed over your chest. Natalie, you're standing as far from her as you possibly can. And Callie—you're in the middle once again. Your aunt did not go through all this trouble to take care of you only to see you at odds like this. And at the very least, her death should bring you back together. Shame on you if you can't see it."

"Uncle Dave, I agree with you," Callie said, then glanced from Natalie to Deanna. "A lot of years have passed. Wasted years. But I thought…I thought Natalie and Deanna were getting beyond their differences."

"So did I," Deanna huffed. "But even though I'm the one who was wronged all those years ago, Natalie is the one acting like the victim."

"Hush!" Uncle Dave hissed, his tone making it clear he was tired of the bickering.

"What happened in the hours I was gone?" Callie couldn't help asking.

"I simply said—"

But Natalie didn't get to finish her statement. Because Uncle Dave quickly interjected, "You think anything you all say about the past matters right now? Your Auntie Jean's dead and gone."

And when his voice cracked, Callie felt a stab of pain in her heart. She glanced in her sisters' directions, noticed that something had changed in their expressions.

They were ashamed. Callie could see that on her sisters' faces.

"My God, I know Jean raised you all to be better than this. To love each other. To forgive."

Neither of the sisters said anything. Because they knew their uncle was right. After all these years, it was time to put aside their differences.

"You're right," Deanna said softly. She looked toward Natalie. "Maybe I…overreacted today. I just thought that once again you were trying to justify what you did, put the blame on me."

Natalie waved a hand. "Deanna, I'm so tired of the fighting. I don't want to rehash everything. That's where we went wrong today…even trying to talk about it. It got us nowhere."

"I agree," Deanna said. She paused briefly, and Callie

noticed her shoulders shake. "What happened between us was a long time ago," Deanna went on. "At the end of the day, you're still my sister. If Auntie Jean dying hasn't made that clear, then nothing will. I want to work to get past everything."

Natalie was the first to move across the room. Deanna walked toward her. Then the two embraced for a long moment, and when they pulled apart, there were tears in each of their eyes.

Callie went over to her sisters and put an arm around each of them, making it a group hug. "Ten years have passed," she said softly. "Ten long years. And this is what brought us together again. A funeral. Uncle Dave's right. It's high time we all get along."

"Now that's more like it," Uncle Dave said, and dabbed at his own eyes. "Your family's all you've really got in this world. If you can't forgive the people who are supposed to be most important to you…"

Callie couldn't help thinking of Nigel, and wondering if he would be able to forgive her for keeping his son from him all these years. She had been important to him.

Once.

But she pushed Nigel out of her mind and concentrated on her sisters. "I know I wasn't specifically a part of your conflict," Callie began, "but I drifted away from you both just the same. I kept my son's paternity from everyone, because I was afraid to trust. I think we all were. And you don't need a trained psychologist to tell us why. It's pretty hard to trust when your own mother abandoned you."

"Speaking of which," Uncle Dave said, "there's something else I want to discuss with you. Something of utmost importance." He got to his feet and walked toward the large maple dresser in his room. "I wanted you all to make your peace before I mentioned this to you."

Callie stared at him, perplexed. "What are you talking about?"

He withdrew an envelope from the dresser. Then he turned back to them, saying, "Your aunt wanted you to have this. But only once she had passed."

"What is it?" Callie asked.

"It has to do with your mother. That's all I know."

Callie's heart began to pound. On one hand she had told herself that she never cared to know anything else about the mother who had abandoned them. Miriam Hart had left them, and that was all there was to it. If their mother had loved them, she never would have walked out of their lives without so much as a glance backward.

But what if there was something else going on? The explanation for *why* she had done what she had done? Was there some reason that would excuse away her neglectful behavior?

Deanna was the one to take the envelope from their uncle and open the flap. She pulled out the two sheets of paper it held and began to read the letter out loud.

"Dear Callie, Deanna and Natalie. I am writing this letter in the event of my passing. I do not believe that secrets should go to the grave with people, not when answers to questions still remain. So that's what this letter is about. Providing answers.

"As you know, your mother brought you to my house one day years ago. She said she would be back for you, but she never returned. Callie, I know that you in particular felt betrayed. Being the oldest, you couldn't understand why your mother wouldn't come back. You had a better grasp of reality than your younger sisters did. And while I don't condone what your mother did, I ask that you try to have some compassion for her.

"Your mother dropped you at my place not because she didn't love you, but because she did. She wanted to protect

you. I don't know the details. All I know is that she was in a
bit of trouble. She didn't even confide in me what that trouble
was, but I suspected it might have involved the law. I had
always expected that she would return. Whether in a few
months, or even a year. But the first year passed, and then
the second, and then the third…and you know the rest. I did
hear from your mother for the first few years every now and
then. She would tell me that she was still unsafe, not giving
me more details than that. She added that she loved you very
much, and said—pleaded with me not to tell you that she
had called because she didn't want to get your hopes up. She
wanted you to know she was coming back only once she was
certain she *could* come back.

"Again, I'm not sure exactly what happened—exactly what
went on with your mother. I do know that she had a boyfriend
at one point that I didn't like. Someone who I saw as trouble.
He could be involved. I'm sorry, I don't remember his name.

"When years passed and I heard nothing more from your
mother, I figured that she was dead. I know I should've
trusted you with this information a long time ago, given you
a more concrete reason as to why she left. But I didn't want
to sour your opinion of her. Callie, with you being so angry,
I thought you could possibly hate your mother if you thought
she'd been involved in something illegal. But I'm telling you
now because if there's a possible chance that she's out there,
I would love for you to be able to find her.

"I will add lastly that your mother absolutely loved you.
No, she wasn't always the best mother, but she did love you.
Sometimes the path we take in this life is not the best one.
We have to pay for our mistakes one way or another. I am
certain that your mother has paid for her mistakes one mil-
lion times over. Because they cost her three little girls who
meant the most in the world to her.

"I love you. And I hope you will have a sense of peace.

I also hope that you will not be angry at me for not sharing this with you before. I stated my reasons, and hope you can understand. God bless you.

"Love, Auntie Jean (Mom)."

Callie took the letter from Deanna's hands after her sister had completed the reading of it. She quickly scanned the very words her sister had read, as if for more confirmation of what she had just heard. It wasn't that she didn't believe it, but there was something in her brain that didn't allow her to accept that it was completely legitimate.

Why would their aunt keep such secrets from them? If she knew their mother had been in some sort of trouble, why hadn't she told them that before? It would have made a lot of difference.

But then another thought came to her. What if their aunt was lying? Wanting to soften the blow of the loss of their mother, she had come up with something to help them feel less guilt, less hurt?

No sooner than that thought came to her, Callie shook her head. No, Auntie Jean wouldn't do something like that to them. Especially not as a deathbed confession.

"What do you think this means?" Deanna asked.

"It means that what we thought was true wasn't," Natalie said, her voice tinged with emotion. "All this time we assumed that Mom ran off and left us because she didn't want to be a mother. That clearly wasn't the case."

Callie found herself shaking her head. She was doubtful. Had their mother been in trouble for over twenty years? "What if Mom gave Auntie Jean a convoluted story?" she asked. "Something to make it seem like what she was doing was okay. Auntie Jean would believe it, of course, but that doesn't make it true."

At Callie's comment, her sisters stared in her direction,

looks of surprise on their faces. "You don't really believe that, do you?" Natalie asked.

Of course Natalie would ask this. She was the youngest, and the one who had held on to the belief that their mother would return for the longest time. "I don't know what to believe," Callie explained. "If Mom was in some sort of trouble, why didn't she tell us about it? And I don't mean when we were younger. But once we got older, she could have reached out to us. She could have sent letters to us. Why insist on keeping us in the dark?"

"What if she couldn't reach out to us?" Deanna suggested. "What if… What if she died?"

The very words sent a chill down Callie's spine. But she knew that the possibility was true.

And yet she didn't want to believe that her mother could have been dead possibly for years, not when she had been so angry with the woman for never returning.

Callie only wished that Auntie Jean had told them about this years earlier. It would have made a difference.

But Callie understood psychology, and wouldn't be surprised if her aunt had feared that they would reject her had she told them the truth before. After having raised them for years, she may have been afraid that she would lose them in some way. That their attention and affection would have suddenly been focused on their lost mother.

Of course, that wouldn't have happened. The girls had seen Auntie Jean as a mother in every sense of the word.

"I think it's important that we try to find out who this man was Auntie Jean was talking about in the letter," Natalie said. "It sounds like he holds the answers to all of this."

"What kind of trouble could she have been in that she didn't want us to know?" Callie asked, still doubtful of the story's verity. "That was so bad that she preferred for us to think she abandoned us?"

"Murder?" Deanna suggested.

Callie's eyes flew to her sister. She wanted to say of course not, that murder was absolutely out of the question. But how did she know?

"We just don't know," Deanna went on.

"And so many years have passed," Callie began, "we might never know what happened to her."

"No," Natalie said. "I can't accept that. I can't accept that I may never know what happened to my mother. We have to find out." She looked at Callie with imploring eyes. "We have to."

"I agree with Natalie," Deanna said, and squeezed Natalie's hand in support. "If there's a chance our mother is out there, we have to do what we can to find her. And if…" Deanna paused, drew in a deep breath. "And if the worst has happened to her, we need to know that, too."

"I know you gave up on our mother a long time ago," Natalie went on. "But what if Auntie Jean was right? What if all this time, she loved us? Loved us and left us to protect us, and perhaps was too ashamed to come back into our lives after all this time?"

Amazing how just a short while ago, Callie had entered this room to find her sisters on opposite sides and not communicating. Now here they were, holding hands, united.

"She could have been honest with us," Callie stressed. "Told us that she was in some sort of trouble."

"If she knew better, she would have done better," Natalie said simply. "Sometimes you just have to forgive people because they didn't know a better way."

Callie let the words sink in. After a moment, she said, "I want to know the truth, too. Whatever it is."

Then she looked around the room, prepared to ask Uncle Dave for his input, but noticed that he had left. He'd left them to read and discuss the letter on their own.

And perhaps he'd left them to continue bonding. Which they were doing. Because after having read the letter that their aunt had written for them, the sisters were suddenly different people. With something to concentrate on, they seemed united for the first time in a long time. So in a way, their aunt's passing had brought them together. Even if it left them with a mystery to solve.

Was what their aunt had written true? That their mother had left them out of love? That she'd been in some kind of trouble and wanted to protect them?

Why hadn't she simply told them the truth? Why had Miriam kept even her sister essentially in the dark?

But even as that question came into Callie's mind, she realized how hypocritical it was. Who was she to talk about being completely forthright, given that she had kept Nigel in the dark about his son for all these years?

Something else suddenly struck her. Callie had found it hard to trust. That much she knew. What if her mother had also found it hard to trust for her own reasons? What if she had gone through something dark in her own past that had shaped her?

"What if Mom went through something," Callie found herself saying. "What if, like us, something happened to her that made her unable to trust? That might explain why she trusted no one—not even her family—with the truth of what was going on in her life."

Natalie stepped forward and took Callie's hand in hers, tears filling her eyes.

"What?" Callie asked. "What's the matter?"

"Nothing's wrong," Natalie said, smiling through her tears. "In fact, hearing you say what you just did—showing some faith in our mother—tells me that finally, everything may be right."

Deanna nodded. "All these years, there's been a big hole in

my life. And it wasn't just because of our mother. When you left and no one heard from you, it broke my heart. But there was a reason for it—you were running from Nigel, and cut us off in the process. It only makes sense that our mother had a reason for doing what she did, even if in the grand scheme of things it wasn't the best one."

"I'm sorry," Callie said. "I know I didn't handle things in the best way. But there was so much going on…you and Natalie fighting and wanting me to pick sides…it seemed easier to run."

"Hey, I'm not trying to blame you for what you did," Deanna said gently. "I know the situation was complicated. But now that we're all together again, able to talk about things, we can finally heal."

"Yes," Natalie agreed. "Deanna's pointing out that there are no more secrets. I know that's how it feels to me. We learned the truth about our nephew, and now we learned that our mother left us with Auntie Jean to protect us. It's a step toward healing. For all of us."

"And speaking of healing, how did things go with Nigel and Kwame today?" Deanna asked.

Callie's stomach twisted. Stepping backward, she lowered herself onto her uncle's bed. "It went well, all things considered."

"Meaning?" Deanna asked.

"He and Kwame hit it off," Callie explained. "It was as if they had known each other for years. They had a great time together."

"That's wonderful," Natalie said.

"Yes," Callie agreed. Her stomach still felt unsettled. Things had gone better than expected, and yet she felt uneasy.

"Then what's the problem?" Natalie asked, sitting beside her on the bed.

What *was* her problem? Certainly Callie couldn't have expected a better outcome than what had happened.

The answer came to her immediately. The reading of their aunt's letter had her thinking of her own mistakes, and how she'd lost someone she had deeply loved. Because instead of fighting for the man she'd loved, she had let a disagreement—albeit a major one—come between them.

"Oh my God," Deanna uttered. "You're still in love with Nigel."

"No," was Callie's immediate reply, but she felt a niggling sensation in her stomach. "Of course I'm not. It's…it's just that seeing him, seeing how well he and Kwame connected, it made me feel enormous regret."

And even if she did still feel something for Nigel, Callie held no illusions that the two of them would reconnect romantically. Too much time had passed for that to happen. She had gone on with her life, and he had gone on with his. And on top of all that, there was her betrayal.

No, the best she could hope for was that she and Nigel were able to get along for the sake of their son. Become friends.

"There may not be hope for me and Nigel," Callie said, facing Natalie, "but what about you and your husband? I heard…I heard you two were having problems."

Natalie scoffed. "Problems? We're over."

Callie made a face. "I don't understand. I thought you and Vance were happy."

"So did I." Natalie shrugged, nonchalant, but her eyes misted. "Surely you heard all about it on the news."

Callie shook her head. "Actually, no. I didn't hear any details. Just that there were problems."

"Well, he couldn't be faithful," Natalie said. "Typical pitfall of the basketball player's wife. I thought he was different, but he wasn't. I can't help feeling stupid for ever trusting him."

Callie saw the way Natalie cast a look toward Deanna, and was certain that Natalie was wondering how Deanna would react to this news. Despite their resolving to put their differences behind them, Callie could only suspect that Natalie assumed Deanna thought she had gotten what she deserved. That her heartbreak because of a cheater was poetic justice.

But Deanna said nothing, for which Callie was grateful. If the sisters were going to make a true effort to get along, they had to leave the past in the past.

"I did hear about your breakup," Deanna said, speaking softly. "On the news. That there was another woman. But you never know if you can believe what you hear though." She paused. "Was he always cheating? Or was it just this one other woman?"

"I don't know if he cheated on me before, but I suspect he did. I couldn't be with him all of the time, and I'm telling you, the women who want a piece of your successful husband are relentless. These women throw themselves at the guys, desperate to hook one. A pregnancy, for example, would be a total coup. They're like vultures. They don't let up."

Callie hoped Natalie wasn't excusing Vance's infidelity, blaming the other woman or women instead of the man who had made vows to her.

"But while I don't know if he was cheating on me all the time, I know that this hurt—big time. Because he cheated with my supposed best friend, Genevieve."

Callie's eyes widened in shock. "Your best friend?"

Natalie shook her head, her expression bitter. "My *former* best friend. We were supposed to be tight. She was one of the first people I met when I moved to Texas. She was the big basketball fan, and dragged me to a lot of the games. I think she secretly hoped to meet one of the players and sail off into the sunset. Instead, I was the one who met Vance…." Natalie's voice trailed off. "I didn't put the pieces together until later that she was jealous. Even though she married soon after I did, she never snagged that high-profile husband. And I think when her marriage ended last year, she made a deliberate play for Vance. She said to me after the fact that if not for her, I never would have met him."

"That's ridiculous," Deanna said. "So because you met Vance while going to games with her, she had a right to betray you?"

Natalie met Deanna's eyes with an expression of surprise. It was clear to Callie that she hadn't expected Deanna to come to her defense.

"Thank you," Natalie said. "It means a lot to hear you say that. Because I know you could easily tell me that I got what I deserved."

"No one deserves that," Deanna said quietly.

"Maybe I did. Because I found out exactly what it feels like to be betrayed by someone close to you. I finally felt what you must have ten years ago."

Deanna said nothing, just nodded. "We're putting the past in the past, remember? That was a long time ago, and I wasn't married to Marvin."

"All the same, I never said this to you before. Even earlier when we argued, I should have said what I've wanted to tell you for a long time. I'm sorry. I'm sorry for what I did…for how I hurt you."

"Thank you," Deanna said.

And then Natalie got to her feet and hugged Deanna, and tears filled Callie's eyes. So much time wasted over the years. All the sisters had drifted apart, and that never should have happened.

"Oh, let me get in there too," Callie said, rising to join her sisters in another group hug.

The hug lingered, one that was ten years overdue.

As they pulled apart, Callie asked, "So, what now regarding your marriage? Have you filed for divorce, or…"

"Or am I hoping to work things out?" Natalie supplied. "Not a chance. Even if I was inclined to forgive him, how could I forgive him for cheating with my friend?" Pausing, Natalie shook her head. "Do you know what my friend had the nerve to say to me? That I'm so beautiful, I can have any guy I want. After I found out what happened, that's what she said to me. She steals my husband, and that's supposed to be my consolation?"

"Jealousy is so ugly," Callie said. "It will make people do things they never thought they would do to you. Even among friends."

"I wasn't jealous of you," Natalie said softly. Now she was looking at Deanna, and the comment clearly had to do with the fact that she had betrayed her sister years before. "I guess I was jealous in a way, jealous because you were spending so much time with Marvin. I missed you in my life. So I did something stupid. I got involved with him, knowing full well that it would never go anywhere, but knowing also that it would drive you and him apart. I was too proud to say that. I let the years come between us. Because of my pride."

"That's behind us now," Deanna said with conviction. And then she reached for Natalie's hand. Callie did the same, taking one of each of her sister's hands into her hand. Three sisters, united again after so many years.

Callie knew it wouldn't necessarily be easy, but they had made it to the other side.

And on this side, things were definitely looking up.

Chapter 8

"Hey, my man," Marshall said as he entered the detectives' office area twenty minutes after Nigel had arrived for their shift.

Nigel made a deliberate show of looking at his watch. "You're late."

"Yeah, I know. I was in court most of the day, then had to rush home and shower. You know the deal." Marshall pulled his chair forward and sank onto it. "What's the latest?"

"I just got off the phone with Garrett Brown's mother," Nigel said. "And we caught a break. She said Garrett's girlfriend confided in her, told her that someone who goes by the street name of Big Boy is the one who killed her son."

"Excellent, excellent."

"I was just about to go through the database, see what I can find out about Big Boy."

"I love it." Marshall moved his chair toward his desk, and

pressed the button to turn on his computer. "I love it when we solve a case in forty-eight hours."

"As you know, even if we put a name to the shooter, the challenge is going to be tracking him down. He could be in the wind right now, on the run."

"We'll get him," Marshall said, and clapped his hands together.

Marshall loved the hunt. When he knew the identity of a killer, he was like a dog with a bone. He didn't let up. Marshall had his goofy moments, but when it came down to it, he was all grit and determination to get killers off the streets.

Marshall turned to him, his eyes growing wide. "Did you meet your son today?"

Nigel nodded, biting his bottom lip as he did. "Yep." And though he felt an unpleasant stirring in his gut when he thought about Callie's betrayal, he also found himself smiling as he thought of Kwame.

"So how did it go, my man? What was it like meeting your son?"

"It was good."

Marshall made a face. "Good?"

"It was more than good," Nigel admitted. "It was incredible." And it had been. He and Callie had created not only a beautiful child, but one who was smart, sensitive and funny.

"Don't keep me in the dark here," Marshall said.

"Kwame's exactly the kind of kid you would want for a son," Nigel elaborated. "Smart, funny. A real good kid. And he loves sports," Nigel added with a grin.

"Dang," Marshall commented, shaking his head. "I still can't believe it. An instant family. I never would've expected Callie to keep your son from you. I always thought she loved you, man."

The comment caused Nigel's jaw to flinch. "Yeah," he concurred softly. "I thought the same thing. Just goes to show…"

In an instant, Nigel's life had changed. Callie's deception had cost him nine years of his son's life, but it had cost him more than that as well. His mother, whose sole goal had been to see him marry and produce offspring, had died never knowing she was a grandparent. His father now lived in Bermuda, having retired there five years ago. He lived with a brother and his wife who'd had a home there for decades. Callie had deprived his parents of time and happiness they could have had with his son.

His father would have to be told of Kwame's existence, hopefully meet him one day. Though he was more frail now after suffering two heart attacks. If anything, Nigel would likely have to head to Bermuda with Kwame in order for his father to meet his grandson.

It struck him as surreal that this was truly his situation, that he was thinking of long-term plans that included a son he had just learned about.

"I hate to say it," Marshall began, "but meeting Kwame... did you get any sense that he might not be your child? I'm not saying Callie would lie about it, but let's face it—if he's yours, she lied to you by omission for all these years."

"He's mine," Nigel said. "I could see it, clear as day."

Remembering the first sight of him, Nigel sucked in a slow breath. He had been stunned at the resemblance. Kwame looked so much like he had when he was his age.

If there had been any doubt, it vanished when he laid eyes on his son. And in that moment of seeing him for the first time, the gravity of his reality had hit him harder than when Callie had dropped her bombshell.

Seeing that he had a son...there were no words to describe it.

"I guess congratulations are in order," Marshall commented. "Aren't you supposed to pass out cigars?"

Nigel knew that Marshall was trying to ease the tension

with his humor, but Nigel wasn't in the mood. He had been thinking about Kwame ever since he and Callie had left, wondering how much time he would have to spend with Kwame before they headed back to Florida.

He was both happy and distressed. Never in his life had he imagined he'd be a father who would be living thousands of miles away from his kid. Though the situation had been awkward, he had been on a high as he had played ball with his son.

But once Callie and Kwame had left, Nigel's mood had plummeted. He had thought about all the years lost, how much his mother would have loved Kwame. So he had paid a visit to his mother's graveside before heading in to work, his mind consumed with regrets over just how excited his mother would have been to be a grandmother.

He had talked to her at the grave as he often did, told her that he had a son. He also told her all the emotions he was feeling—from anger, to confusion, to love, to fear. He could picture Edna Williams listening to him from above, her classic maternal expression of understanding on her beautiful face.

And as he got back into his car, it was thoughts of his mother that had him doing his best to push the regrets and disappointment aside. Having gone to talk to his mother reminded him of one thing he knew she would tell him if she were alive. She would tell him not to hold on to the anger.

His mother always said there was no point in crying over spilt milk, no matter how big the mess was. You just had to clean it up and move on.

"This isn't how I planned things," Nigel said to Marshall, "but it is what it is. A lot of men never get an opportunity to be a father, so I have to count my blessings, right?"

"You're my hero, man," Marshall said. "A better man than me, that's for sure."

"I'm not going to turn my back on Kwame," Nigel said.

"Next thing, you're going to be handing out wedding invitations," Marshall said.

Nigel felt a jolt to the chest at Marshall's words.

"Don't look so shocked," Marshall went on when Nigel didn't speak. "I know how much you loved Callie."

Nigel's chest felt tight, making it hard to breathe. Yes, he'd loved Callie, God knew he had. But the only thing allowing him to go forward and embrace being a father to Kwame was trying to block Callie's deception from his mind.

Because damn, seeing her again…there had been a part of him that had wanted her still.

Even with a bandage on her forehead and a sling on her arm, she was breathtaking. And the fact that she'd been hurt had brought out his protective instincts even more.

But he had to rein them in. Because Callie was not deserving of his protection. He didn't want to think about taking care of her. She was no longer deserving of his love.

Nigel stood. "Time to canvass the neighborhood, see if we can find Big Boy."

"I thought you were going to look up the information in the database," Marshall said.

That had been the plan, but Nigel could no longer sit still. He needed to get up, get moving.

It was the only thing he could do to help clear his mind of thoughts of Callie.

Callie's mind was on the letter her aunt had written as she had left the house to take a walk. It was something she'd done often as a teen, the nearby park with its lush trees and dazzling array of flowers the perfect spot for her to sit and think.

So much had happened today. First seeing Nigel, and introducing him to Kwame. Then, learning that their aunt had kept the truth about their mother from them all these years.

Callie had sat and pondered everything for a good long while, needing solitude to think. Oddly, her thoughts kept coming back to Nigel. Thinking of him today—how incredibly sexy he had looked—had her heart beating faster.

Which she didn't understand at all. For God's sake, ten years had passed since she'd last seen him.

But she couldn't deny the reaction, not even now as she found her skin feeling flush. The undeniable truth was that her body still reacted to his.

She remembered the jolt she'd felt when she had walked back outside with the drinks for Nigel and Kwame, and seeing that he had taken his shirt off. There had been the raw, female reaction to his strong male physique.

But what haunted her, even now, was that scar on his chest. It was the kind of scar that spoke to either a serious health issue, or a violent trauma.

"Stop doing this," Callie told herself. "Stop thinking about Nigel."

But as she got up and started to walk out of the park, she heard a voice in her head say, *Easier said than done.*

Kwame's eyes lit up when he saw his mother enter the front door. He was in the living room, holding the controller for the Wii game, but promptly dropped it and rushed toward her. He gave her a big hug, mindful not to hurt her injured arm.

Callie would never tire of his reaction to her. People told her that as he got older, he wouldn't want to lavish her with affection because he would be more conscious of his male image. But knowing Kwame's sweet demeanor, she couldn't imagine that day coming.

And if it did, all the more reason to enjoy her son's loving attention now.

"How've you been, sweetie?" she asked, running a hand over his head. She had been gone about an hour and a half. "Your aunts treating you well?"

"They're awesome!" Kwame exclaimed. "We've been playing ever since you left."

"Aah," Callie said, understanding. She threw a look at Deanna, who shrugged sheepishly. Well, she could hardly be unhappy with her sisters for spending time with Kwame, even if they were playing video games.

They had nine years to make up for.

"Auntie Deanna loves being Snake," Kwame went on.

Again, Deanna shrugged. "I have no clue what I'm doing. I'm just pressing buttons on a remote. And speaking of which, it's your turn." She passed the remote to Natalie, who looked as confused as Callie felt every time she played Super Smash Bros. with her son.

"I'll leave you to it," Callie said.

"If you want to play," Natalie said, "feel free."

Callie exchanged a knowing look with her sister, one that said *Not a chance.* It wasn't that she wouldn't or couldn't play. It was that this particular game she understood as well as she understood the Russian language.

So Callie escaped upstairs, where she took her arm out of the sling and tried to move it. It still hurt, but not as badly as it did last week. But she simply couldn't move her arm the way she liked, and knew it was too soon to push it. She hated being restricted, and hoped she wouldn't need the sling that much longer.

Callie was surprised when she heard the door open, and even more surprised when she saw Kwame standing at the door.

"Hey," Callie said, smiling. "I thought you were playing the Wii game with your aunts."

"I wanted to check on you," Kwame said, and Callie could see the hint of worry in his eyes. "Are you okay?"

"Yes." Callie opened her good arm to her son. "I'm fine, sweetheart. What about you?"

"I'm good."

Callie hadn't had a real chance to talk to him since their return from his father's. So she took his hand and led him to the bed, where they both sat.

"Did you have a good day, son?" Callie asked, trailing her fingers over his forehead. "Meeting your father, I mean?"

The boy's smile was instantaneous. "I had a great day."

"And you have no questions for me? Nothing else you want to know? About anything." She assumed he would still have questions for her later, even perhaps be angry with her once he got over this initial phase of excitement about learning that his father was alive.

"All that really matters is that my dad is alive, and that he loves me," Kwame said.

Callie's eyes misted, but she tried not to let the tears fall. In that simple statement, her son was letting her know that he forgave her, that he was looking at the big picture.

It made Callie think once again about the letter her aunt had left her and her sisters. How her own mother had been in some kind of trouble and had fled. Couldn't she have sat Callie down and reasonably explained to her what was going on? Explain that there was some sort of trouble, that she loved them and had to leave them for a while? Callie had been eight. Old enough to get the jist of a serious conversation.

The very fact that Kwame was being so forgiving made it clear that kids simply needed to be told the truth. Adults often doubted a child's ability to handle the truth, but children were stronger than people thought.

Thinking of their mother, Callie felt the familiar anxiety.

The pain. That sense of abandonment that was like nothing else.

And then she remembered Natalie's comment. That if their mother knew better, she would have done better.

Natalie was ready to forgive, no question. But there had to be other ways to parent than to leave your kids in the dark in an effort to protect—

The thought died abruptly. Callie caught herself, and was ashamed. Maybe she ought to be more like Natalie, willing to forgive. Because hadn't she kept her son in the dark regarding the truth about his father?

No, she hadn't outright lied to Kwame, but she hadn't been truthful either. Her son had been left to fill in the blanks, and had assumed that his father was dead.

While Callie could perhaps forgive her mother for keeping her secrets, what she wasn't yet ready to forgive her for was the bigger crime: abandoning her and her sisters. The fact that she'd been in touch with their aunt for at least a few years meant she could have sent letters for her own daughters, if not called.

She had chosen to stay away.

That was what hurt the most.

And if she was still alive today, yet had stayed away all these years…well, how could her mother explain that in a way that would absolve her guilt?

Yes, Callie had made her share of mistakes. She hadn't been a perfect parent. But as she pulled Kwame against her body, she knew that she'd done at least one thing right. She had raised a warm and caring young man.

"When do I see Dad again?" Kwame asked.

"Um, I don't know. Maybe tomorrow?"

"When do we go back to Florida?"

"I haven't booked our return trip home," Callie said.

Kwame smiled. "Good."

"Good?" Callie questioned.

"I want to spend as much time with Dad as possible."

Callie nodded. "Of course. And you will."

"Can we call Dad now?" Kwame asked.

"He's working, remember?"

Kwame frowned slightly.

"Don't worry. We'll call him in the morning."

"Okay." Kwame rose from the bed. "I'm gonna go back downstairs. I have to finish my game."

"You do that."

And as Kwame bounded out of the room, Callie realized her conundrum. She couldn't simply leave and head back to Florida, go on with her life as she had known it.

Because like it or not, her life once again included Nigel.

And in a way that she would never have anticipated ten years ago.

Ten years ago, she always thought that if she and Nigel were to have children, they would be a married, loving couple.

But life didn't always work out the way a person planned. Callie knew that better than anyone else.

Chapter 9

The next afternoon, the phone rang shortly after Callie and her family had eaten lunch. Callie had her good hand in a sink of soapy water, where she was helping to place the dirty lunch dishes. Natalie, who was closest to the wall phone, answered it.

"Oh, sure," she said into the receiver. "She's right here." Placing the phone against her chest, Natalie said, "Callie, it's for you."

"Who is it?"

"Nigel."

Callie's heart slammed against her chest. Why was it that she should react this way, simply hearing that he was on the line?

She dried her hands on a dish towel, then walked to the wall where the phone was. She accepted the receiver from Natalie. "Hello?"

"I was wondering if you and Kwame are free this evening," Nigel said without preamble.

"We don't have any specific plans."

"Then how about you come over here? I'd really like to spend more time with my...my son."

"Sure," Callie said. She could tell by Nigel's voice that it was taking some getting used to the idea of being a father which was beyond understandable. "I think he would be happy to do that as well."

"I have some errands to run, but I'll be home about five. Is that a good time?"

"As good as any," Callie said.

"I'll see you then. I figure we can order a pizza and watch a couple movies."

Nigel spoke in a somewhat dispassionate tone, and Callie felt uneasy. But it was becoming clear to her just how awkward this would be for her. For her and Nigel to communicate, relate to each other, hang out with their son as a family.

She forced a smile. "Sounds like a plan."

"Are you seeing Nigel again today?" Natalie asked as Callie placed the phone on the wall mount.

Callie nodded. "Yeah. He wants us to come over this evening."

Natalie's eyes rose, hopeful. But she said nothing.

She didn't need to. Callie knew that Natalie was ever the romantic, and she clearly had ideas about her and Nigel reconnecting.

Leaving Natalie in the kitchen, Callie headed out the doors to the backyard, where Deanna and Uncle Dave were sitting at the patio table, all drinking tall glasses of lemonade. It was the kind of day for relaxing and having a cookout. Within a couple hours, she had no doubt that someone would fire up the grill.

As if Deanna had read her mind, she said, "It's such a

lovely day, I think we should grill some steaks later. Or burgers. I have the best recipe for barbecue burgers you've ever tasted. I was just telling Uncle Dave that I'm planning to head out to the store fairly soon to pick up the ingredients. Maybe we can even have some other family members come over. We can share stories about Auntie Jean."

"Oh, that sounds like a very nice idea," Callie said, knowing it might especially help to perk up Uncle Dave's spirits. "But I just spoke with Nigel. He was suggesting that Kwame and I come over this evening."

"Tell him to come on over here," Deanna said. "He can join us. The more the merrier."

Callie thought about that, and had no objection to it. But she knew that in the early stage of bonding, it was probably best for Kwame to spend time with Nigel alone. She wasn't certain that Nigel would be ready for any family get-togethers as of yet.

"It's probably best for another day," Callie said. "In fact, I can suggest it to Nigel. It can be something we work toward."

"We can plan the cookout for another day," Deanna suggested. "If you and Kwame won't be here—"

"No, don't put it off. Call the family. See if they're free to stop by. It's a great idea, isn't it, Uncle Dave?"

"Your Auntie Jean always loved filling this house with food and people."

"There you go," Callie said, aware that she sounded a little too chipper.

Deanna approached her, said in a whisper, "Are you okay?"

No, I'm not okay. I feel as if I'm in the twilight zone. But she said, "Yeah, sure. I'm perfectly fine."

But the truth was, Callie wasn't fine. Because the very idea of seeing Nigel again had her stomach tickling with nerves.

It was uncomfortable, seeing Nigel like this, being amicable, when at one time they had hardly been able to see each other without ripping off their clothes.

But this was her own fault. She was the one who had created this awkward circumstance by not being honest.

She had no choice but to deal with the discomfort.

Nigel opened the door, took one look at Callie and found his gut clenching. Dear God in heaven, what was she trying to do to him?

As much as he had told himself not to think about her, that he would deal with her only because it was necessary in order to forge a relationship with his son, seeing her now made it clear he could hardly forget her. In fact, he wondered if she had dressed to get his attention, because she was undeniably hot.

She was wearing a low-cut sundress that hung to the ground, showing off cleavage he didn't remember her having as well as a figure that had become more womanly. The glittery flip-flops she wore highlighted just how pretty her feet were. Feet with high arches he had used to enjoy rubbing.

"Hi," Callie said, in a faint voice that Nigel was sure held suggestive overtones.

She had done her makeup. Nigel wasn't even seeing the bandage or the sling. All he was seeing was one sexy woman.

Nigel cleared his throat. "Hi. Glad you could make it."

Kwame stepped forward and placed his arms around his waist. "Hi, Dad."

Hi, Dad. Those words hit him, hit him hard. This moment was so surreal.

Kwame released him, and Nigel walked into the house. Callie and Kwame followed him into the living room.

"Do you like pizza?" Nigel asked.

"I love pizza," Kwame responded, his eyes lighting up.

Nigel looked from him to Callie. He almost expected her

to protest. He wouldn't be surprised to learn that she was a militant mom. The type who would be quick to point out that a pizza loaded with fattening toppings wasn't good for her son. The kind of mother who would balk at daycare workers or dental hygienists offering her son a lollipop.

But Callie said nothing, just stood there with that sexy dress that Nigel couldn't help wondering if she had put on for his benefit.

He had to wrench his gaze away from her. He shouldn't be feeling any sort of sexual attraction to her. Clearly he was suffering from a bout of insanity.

"What do you like on your pizza?" Nigel asked Kwame.

"Pepperoni."

"Pepperoni, of course. Everybody's favorite."

"I like mushrooms, too," Kwame pointed out.

"And black olives," Callie chimed in.

Nigel looked at her. He was suddenly struck with a profound feeling. One he couldn't quite place. One beyond the obvious physical attraction he was feeling for her.

Because here he was, with the woman who had left him years ago, and they were doing what an ordinary family would do on any given evening.

Ordering pizza.

And yet there was nothing ordinary about them. The situation was unusual, to say the obvious.

At least he was glad to know that she wasn't too overly protective of Kwame and what he ate. Because one of the things that Nigel wanted to do was take Kwame to an amusement park and buy him one of those giant waffles smothered with ice cream and strawberries. As a child, Nigel's parents had always said no to him having that kind of a treat when they were out, and he'd always known that when he became a father he would do the exact opposite.

Callie met his eyes, then she glanced away. And again,

Nigel felt that rush of attraction for her. He wondered what she was thinking.

Nigel started toward the table that held the phone. "So, a pizza with pepperoni, mushrooms and olives. And what about anchovies, Kwame? Do you like those?"

The boy's grimace was instantaneous. "Ewww! No way!"

Nigel grinned. He didn't like anchovies, either. He had simply been messing with Kwame, trying to create a fun moment. He remembered all too well how, when he had been young, his parents had always ordered anchovies on their pizza. It had ruined every pizza for him.

It wasn't that Nigel had had the worst upbringing, but he'd always been mindful when he was a kid that there were things he would do differently when he became a dad. He had looked forward to being a father, but just hadn't met anyone he wanted to father a child with.

Except for Callie.

As Nigel's hand reached for the receiver, he swallowed. A lump had lodged in his throat. In so many ways, this was what he'd always wanted. A family. And with this woman.

Yet Callie had taken it away from him.

She could come here looking sexy and sweet and oh-so-tempting, but that wouldn't erase her betrayal.

Nigel knew he couldn't hang on to the past, that for the sake of getting to know his son he had to put aside his feelings of hurt and betrayal.

He lifted the receiver, but didn't punch in the number for the pizza establishment. Instead, he was wondering if Callie had ever loved him the way he had loved her. Because if she had, how could she have deceived him like this?

Nigel's stomach twisted with the thought, and he remembered vividly those nights when she had first left, the anxiety he'd felt as he'd lain in bed. How desperately he'd wished that she would call him, allow them to work things out.

But she never had.

Nigel expelled a breath. He didn't want to go there. He didn't want to take a mental trip down memory lane to a place that held only bad memories. So he made the call, ordered an extra large pizza and some sodas.

Then he made his way back to the living room. "What about a movie, bud?" he asked Kwame.

"That'd be awesome. I love your TV."

Nigel looked toward the forty-two-inch flat-screen television. "If you like that, wait until you see the basement."

"What's in the basement?"

"Come see."

Nigel led the way across the living room, and opened the door that led to the basement. Moments later, they were all downstairs. Beyond the basement living room was another door that Nigel opened. And when Kwame stepped into that room, he said, "Wow!"

"A home theater?" Callie asked, also sounding impressed.

Kwame surged forward. "Look at all these movies! There must be two hundred in here!"

"Three hundred twenty and counting," Nigel said. "This home theater was my one splurge when I finished renovating this place. Sixty-inch television, awesome surround sound. It's pretty impressive."

"That's for sure!" Kwame commented.

"As you can see, I love my movies." Nigel gestured to the built-in shelving filled with DVD cases. "But it's always nicer to watch movies with someone, rather than alone."

"Have you watched all of them?" Kwame asked.

"A lot, but not all."

Callie moved toward him, a smile on her face. "You really did a magnificent job with the renovations. You did this all yourself?"

Nigel nodded, his breath catching in his throat. The

multicolored pattern on her dress—purple, red and pink swirls—looked outstanding against her dark skin. And that smile…it radiated from the inside out, the way it had when she used to smile at him ten years ago.

"Yes I did," Nigel told her.

"It's lovely, Nigel. Truly lovely."

And for some insane reason, it pleased him to know that she liked the work he had done here.

Then, regaining his wits, he turned away from her, needing to break the spell that seemed to come over him whenever he looked into her eyes. Because he didn't want to remember that fiery young woman he had loved. Remembering the woman he'd loved would only lead him to remembering how hurt he'd been when she had left.

"Pizza and a movie in this home theater," Callie said, moving toward one of the built-in shelves. "That'll be an awesome night, won't it, Kwame?"

"For sure."

Nigel walked to a shelf on the opposite wall and began to peruse his extensive DVD collection. He was looking for something that Kwame might like. He had hundreds of movies, but not a lot that would be appropriate for a nine-year-old. He hadn't had a child, so hadn't stocked up on kid movies, but that would have to change. He would go out with Kwame and pick out a number of movies.

"If you don't see a movie you like here, I've also got a subscription to Netflix, so we can order one to watch if you like."

"Oh, *Iron Man*!" Kwame exclaimed. "I want to see this."

Looking at his son, seeing his excitement, all the work he had put into this place suddenly meant even more to him. He felt an overwhelming sense of joy that he was able to make his son happy by providing him the experience of a home theater.

"Is *Iron Man* okay?" Nigel asked Callie.

"It's fine. He's already seen it, and loved it."

"And then we can watch the second one," Kwame added.

"Likely not both for today, Kwame," Callie told him. "But you can certainly come back another day and watch another movie. I'm sure your father won't mind."

"Of course I won't mind," Nigel said.

Kwame came over to him and wrapped his arms around his chest. "Thanks, Dad."

Would Nigel ever get used to the name *Dad*? Hearing Kwame call him that touched him on the deepest level. "No problem, son. No problem at all."

After watching *Iron Man*, Kwame asked if they could shoot more hoops, so they all headed outside. Shooting hoops led to throwing a football in the backyard, and after an hour and a half, they then went back inside because Kwame again insisted they all watch *Iron Man 2*.

"It's already getting late," Callie said. "We've taken up enough of your father's time."

"No problem with me if he wants to watch another movie," Nigel said. "Unless you've got to get going."

"Please, Mom?"

A moment later, Callie nodded. "All right. But any time you're sick of us, let us know."

"Sick of you?" Nigel countered. "I'm getting to know my son. I'm never going to get sick of this."

Callie hadn't been serious, had said the words as a joke, but now realized how insensitive they were.

The truth was, she had hoped that Nigel would tell them they had to leave. He had been giving her odd looks all evening, looks that had her skin burning up. Because she would swear that he was looking at her as if he wanted to get her naked.

"I didn't mean that the way it sounded," Callie said. "It's just that I know you've got work—"

"I've taken a leave of absence," Nigel said simply.

"What?"

"I want to spend as much time as possible with Kwame," was his simple reply.

And so they watched *Iron Man 2*, and when Kwame fell asleep on one of the leather chairs, Nigel said, "No point waking him up. I'll just bring him to the bedroom I built in the basement."

"Nigel, you don't have to. It's late. We can leave."

"It's late, and I've got the room. There's no reason you can't stay."

There's every reason not to stay! Callie's mind screamed. With Kwame asleep, what was she to do? Spend time with Nigel *alone*?

She couldn't…

And yet, she didn't protest as Nigel lifted Kwame into his arms. What was she to say? She knew better than anyone that when Kwame conked out, nothing could wake him.

Feeling helpless, Callie stood in the home theater, watching as Nigel took their sleeping son out of the room. Once Nigel was out the door, he looked over his shoulder at her. "Can you come with me? I'll need help opening the door."

Callie's heart beat faster, which was ridiculous. It was the knowing that she and Nigel were about to be alone….

She followed Nigel to another door in the basement and, when he nodded at her, she opened it. Using his shoulder, he flicked on the light, revealing a double bed and a tastefully decorated room.

Callie quickly scurried ahead and pulled down the white bedspread. Then Nigel laid Kwame on the sheets.

Oh God, what now? her mind screamed.

Nigel turned toward her, and damn if he didn't level

another one of those looks on her. He had been assessing her in a purely sexual way ever since she had arrived.

But wasn't that what she wanted? Why else had she made sure to wear an outfit that revealed her cleavage and highlighted her figure?

Callie stood rooted to the spot as Nigel walked past her out the room. Not for the first time this evening, she caught a whiff of his cologne. Old Spice. She recognized it from ten years ago when he used to wear it.

A memory of her burying her nose in his neck flashed into her mind. Oh, how much she had enjoyed—

"Are you coming?" Nigel asked.

Callie was suddenly flushed, jarred from her erotic memory. And as she looked at Nigel, her heart began to pound furiously, as though he had just asked her if she was going to join him in his bed.

Chapter 10

"Are you coming?" Nigel repeated.

Nigel stood at the foot of the stairs, staring at her. He had to be wondering what was wrong with her, why she wasn't moving.

"Yeah," she finally said. "Just give me a second."

And then she leaned forward and kissed Kwame on the forehead, as if that had been why she had been delaying her exit from the room.

Upstairs, Callie followed Nigel into the living room. When he stopped, she said, "If you want me to leave, I'm fine with that. I can come back for Kwame in the—"

"You want to leave. Why am I not surprised?"

Callie would have to have been deaf to miss out on the sarcasm dripping from Nigel's voice. "I'm just saying...I get that me being here is about you getting to know Kwame. He's down for the night, I can tell you that. So—"

"And what about us?" Nigel asked.

Callie's heart sped up. "Excuse me?"

"We're parents. Like it or not, we're going to have to forge a friendship."

"I…you think I'm running from being friends with you?"

Nigel shrugged. "Aren't you?"

"I…" Callie didn't know what to say. Because she certainly knew that was how it must seem.

"After all we meant to each other, the least we can do is sit down and talk. You can fill in some of the blanks for me. Kwame's first word, how old he was when he walked…all that stuff."

Was that what he really wanted? As far as Callie saw it, hearing the milestones in Kwame's life might be more hurtful to him. Remind him of all he'd missed out on.

But she said, "I'll tell you anything you want to know." Then she sighed. "Do you have any wine?"

Nigel nodded. "I've got something in the fridge. I'll be back in a second."

Callie took a seat on the sofa, and less than a minute later, Nigel was back with a glass of white wine. He extended it to her, and she sipped it immediately. It had a slightly sweet flavor, and was refreshing.

When she looked up, she found Nigel staring at her, as though studying her. She could hardly stand his intense scrutiny!

So she broke the silence. "I've got online storage where I keep backups of important documents, photos and the like. I've got pictures of Kwame ever since he was a baby there. I can show you the various albums of his growth over the years."

Finally, Nigel's eyes lit up. "I'd like that."

Callie took another sip of wine as he disappeared into the bedroom. Moments later, he was back with his laptop.

He fired it up and then passed it to her. Callie logged on to the website that offered her online storage. This was the first time she had found it useful in this way, because until now she always accessed these files from her home computer.

She quickly found her pictures folder and the various sub-folders, and opened up the first one. She had scanned all the photos from Kwame's birth and they were readily accessible.

"He was eight pounds, two ounces," Callie explained, looking at a photo of her holding him moments after his birth. Tamara had been in the delivery room with her, and had been the one to take the picture.

"Where are your sisters?" Nigel asked after she went through about fifteen photos. "Your aunt and uncle?"

Callie exhaled harshly. "It wasn't only you I kept in the dark. I didn't tell any of my family about the baby. I was young, still in school…and I guess I was worried they would judge me. I eventually told my aunt and uncle, but I hadn't been talking to my sisters. I know they heard, but they didn't learn the truth about everything until I came back home for the funeral."

Nigel looked at her, nodded and then glanced back at the computer. If he wanted to ask her about her estrangement from her sisters, he refrained.

He went through the different albums: Kwame's first birthday, Kwame riding a bike, Kwame's first day of school. Callie answered the questions he had, but he became more silent as he went through the photos of Kwame as an older boy, and she could only imagine that he was feeling a mix of emotions.

She could see it in his body language, and could tell that he was holding in his emotions. It wouldn't surprise her to know that he might want to give her a piece of his mind.

These photos…precious memories…were more proof of everything he had missed out on.

"I know I can't change the past," Callie said softly, "but I vow to do right by you and Kwame. You have my word. I will do everything in my power to make sure that you spend as much time together as possible."

Callie's voice trailed off as Nigel looked away. She saw his Adam's apple rise and fall. The tension between them was so thick, she could cut it with a knife.

"Can I ask you something?" Callie began, needing to change the subject.

"Sure," Nigel said.

"Yesterday…when I came outside and saw you with your shirt off, I noticed that you had a pretty thick scar down the center of your chest."

Nigel pulled his T-shirt upward. "You mean this?"

Callie placed a hand on her chest when she saw the scar. Up close, it looked vicious. Whatever had happened, Nigel had gone through something horrific.

"Yes. That."

Nigel did something Callie didn't expect. He pulled the T-shirt over his head. Let her get a good look at the angry scar.

"What happened to you?" she asked.

"I was shot."

Callie gasped slightly at the admission, and then her heart began to pound. Suddenly she was imagining how differently things might have been had Nigel been killed in the line of duty. Killed long before he ever had a chance to know he was a father.

It was a hard thought to bear. As difficult as it was right now being here in the aftermath of admitting that she had kept a very big secret from him for years, it was important to accept whatever negative repercussions that came as a result of her actions. And the reality was, Nigel could have died without ever knowing that he was a father. She was going to deal with the weight of that truth for a long time.

"What—what happened?" Callie asked, her voice stuttering.

"I was on the job," Nigel explained. "Working the case of a guy who had killed his wife and two children. We had a lead on him, found him. He ran, so we gave chase. He wasn't about to be captured, so he started firing. I got hit." Nigel shrugged.

He had recited these life-altering facts as though telling her what he wanted her to pick up from Winn-Dixie. It was unnerving.

Callie remembered a time when she could have lain in his arms and he would have told her everything, with emotion filling his heart. Because he had cared for her deeply. He had trusted her with his heart.

But that had changed.

Callie swallowed the lump that had lodged in her throat. She didn't like the situation they were in, but there was no point in looking down memory lane at the past. What was done was done. She couldn't turn back the clock. She could only do what she was doing now—try to rectify the situation.

She found herself easing her finger forward and touching the mangled skin. She hadn't expected to, and she felt an electric charge when her fingers touched Nigel's body. After all this time, she felt something for him.

She tried to ignore the sensations whirling within her and asked, "How close to your heart were you hit?"

"Six millimeters to the left, and I wouldn't be here," Nigel explained calmly.

Callie drew back her hand as though shocked by a live wire. The confirmation that indeed he could have died resonated with her more than ever. "What?"

"If the bullet had struck me six millimeters to the left, it would have hit my aorta, and I would have bled out. If it had struck me a couple of inches lower, the bullet would have pierced my heart. As it was, I was struck in the left subclavian vein. The doctors had to operate on me for over five hours to save my life."

As though she was the one who had been shot, pain pierced Callie's heart. "And the criminal?" she asked when she was able to catch her breath. "What happened to him?"

"He was shot and killed."

"You shot him?"

"No, not me. My partner. Once I was hit, my partner returned fire and killed him."

What he must have gone through! He'd put his life on the line to serve and protect, and had almost paid the ultimate price.

Callie remembered all too well how they had not seen eye to eye on issues in the past. Back then, she'd been so angry with the police because one bad officer had beaten her friend so horribly that it had cost him his life. But she was older and wiser, and had to concede that as a police officer, Nigel was doing good work. Cops put their lives on the line every single day, something she could appreciate now.

How narrow-minded she had been to look at all of the police force in such a bad light. Yes, there were bad cops out there. Too many of them, she knew. People in roles of authority should be able to be trusted, and sadly couldn't be. But just because there were bad apples in the bunch didn't mean you could paint everyone with the same brush.

"I'm glad you're okay," Callie said, her voice barely a whisper.

"Are you?"

At the question, Callie's lips parted in surprise. "Of course I am."

"If I died, you would've been able to keep your secret forever. I would have never been the wiser."

"And that's exactly why I'm happy you're here. Because

you had a right to know. It would have been a crime if you had died without knowing that you had fathered a child."

"Hmm."

Callie got to her feet. She began to pace. "I see now how happy Kwame is. It's so clear that he's needed you in his life all along. I...I'm so sorry."

Nigel stared up at her, his lips pulled in a tight line. He looked angry.

So Callie couldn't have been more startled when he suddenly got to his feet, stepped in front of her and slipped his fingers into her hair. "Do you know how many days I wondered if you would come back to me?" he asked, his hot breath fanning her face. "Do you know how many times I wished you hadn't walked out on me?"

Callie couldn't speak. All she could register was the furious pounding of her heart as she wondered if Nigel was going to kiss her.

Did she want that?

The fact that her body felt more alive than ever made it clear that she *did* want it.

"I wanted to do this so many times," he said, trailing one finger down her cheek, creating a path of fire. "But you never gave me the chance. Because you never came back."

Callie couldn't speak. Suddenly, desire was pulsing through her veins.

Nigel's mouth came down on hers, hard. Her body erupted in an immediate firestorm of passion. He kissed her with an urgent need that matched all the raging sensations inside her. Kissing Nigel, it was as though no time had passed at all.

And all too soon, it was over. Nigel broke the kiss and pulled away from her, leaving her feeling as though he'd thrown a glass of cold water on her.

"Did you think of me?" Nigel asked, almost an accusing tone in his voice—a stark contrast to when he had gathered her in his arms. "Did you ever think of me and regret what you did?"

"Of course. More than you know."

Nigel moved away from her, and Callie was breathless. One minute she had been ready to take off her clothes, and she sensed that Nigel had been in the exact state of mind. The next he was turning his back on her.

"Second door on the right is a spare bedroom. You can sleep there."

That was it?

"I'm heading out," Nigel said, not even turning to face her before he disappeared through the front door.

For a long time after Nigel left, Callie sat in the living room of his home, feeling dazed, confused and downright awful. What had happened between them?

How was it that they had gone from talking to kissing? And why on earth did she continue to feel a rush of excitement when she thought of Nigel planting his mouth on hers?

She wasn't interested in rekindling her relationship with Nigel. Too much time had passed for that, and she certainly knew that he didn't trust her, maybe didn't even like her anymore.

So why on God's green earth had he kissed her?

And God help her, there was still fire when he touched her. That same undeniable spark that had existed between the two of them years ago clearly hadn't died.

Or maybe what she was truly feeling was regret. Regret over what could have been.

As if! She had clearly been turned on, and had wanted Nigel to do more than kiss her.

Obviously it's been too long since you got any, she thought sourly.

She reached for the wine glass, finished it off. Then glanced at the clock. Nigel had been gone for twenty minutes.

For the first time, she found herself wondering if he had a girlfriend. He didn't have a wife, that much was clear. But what if he had run straight into the arms of a nurturing girlfriend?

The thought made Callie's stomach clench painfully. She didn't want to think that Nigel could kiss her like that, then go spend time with another woman.

"Seriously, Callie—what's gotten into you?"

She got up from the sofa and went to the kitchen, where she poured herself more wine. She needed it, if for no other reason than to help her fall asleep.

And as the next thirty minutes passed and still no Nigel, Callie felt even worse.

Regret. That kiss—all fire and need—was causing her to wonder how things would have been had she not left Nigel ten years ago.

And yet, Callie knew that there was no point in regretting anything.

Ultimately, that kind of thinking did a person no good. Callie knew better than anyone that wondering how things might have played out differently with Nigel was a recipe for heartache. Just as it had been for her to wonder about her mother all those years. What was done was done, and all she could do now was move forward. And moving forward meant giving her son a chance to get to know his father.

As to why Nigel had kissed her, Callie suddenly knew the answer. He wanted to give her a taste of what she'd missed out on.

And it had been effective, but as Callie headed to the kitchen with her empty wine glass, she was determined not to dwell on the path she hadn't chosen.

There were more important things to consider, like

working out a custody arrangement before she and Kwame headed back to Florida. Thankfully, the school year was about to end in Miami, which meant Callie could spend a couple months in Cleveland if need be. And even if she had to get back home, Kwame could stick around if Nigel agreed. It would be a great opportunity for them to get to know each other better.

And from here on in, Callie and Nigel could work out a custody agreement that would allow him to spend lots of time with his son. A good portion of the summer break, alternate Christmases. Easter. Spring break.

She had meant what she'd said to Nigel. That she would do right by him and Kwame. She wouldn't rip her son from Nigel's life a second time.

Callie had checked on Kwame, who was still out cold, then tried to make herself as comfortable as possible. Just like the spare bedroom in the basement, this one was tastefully decorated in neutral colors.

In the bathroom, Callie found extra packages of toothbrushes, for which she was glad. She didn't have the night clothes she would normally sleep in, but she found an oversized T-shirt in the drawer in the second bedroom and helped herself to it.

Ready for bed, she glanced at the clock. An hour and a half had passed since Nigel had left. It was after eleven-thirty, and he still wasn't home.

Callie closed her eyes, but she simply couldn't sleep. She found herself reaching into her purse and taking out her cell phone. She had turned it off, not wanting any interruptions and not expecting any important calls. But she powered it on now, knowing that she needed to talk to a friend about all that had transpired.

It was late, but she called Tamara's number, hoping her

friend picked up. She was the one person who knew all her secrets.

"Callie?" Tamara said when she answered the phone.

"Hey, girl. Yeah, it's me."

"I've been waiting to hear from you," Tamara said, and Callie could hear a tinge of concern in her voice. "How are you?"

Callie knew Tamara was referring to her injuries…injuries that had come about because of Tamara's husband. "I'm okay. My arm still hurts, and has limited movement, but I'll survive."

"Gosh, I feel so bad. Patrick…I think he just doesn't know how to handle us being apart."

"Mmm," was all Callie said, because she wasn't interested in hearing Tamara excuse Patrick for running her off the road. As far as Callie was concerned, the man was dangerously unstable.

"How did the funeral go?" Tamara asked.

"It was hard. Seeing my Auntie Jean in the casket, knowing I had wasted so many years staying away…" Callie swallowed, went on. "It was hard."

"What about your sisters?"

"That was the one good thing. Seeing them. And Uncle Dave, of course. My aunt's funeral put everything in perspective, and we're now all working at getting over our differences."

"That sounds great, Callie."

"Yeah," Callie said softly. "So far so good."

"What about Nigel?" Tamara asked. "Did you get to talk to him like you wanted to?"

"Actually, I did."

A full five seconds passed. Then Tamara said, "Oh no you don't. You're not going to clam up now. Tell me the details! How did it go, telling him he has a son?"

"It went pretty well, actually." Callie's stomach fluttered, thinking of how easily Nigel and Kwame had bonded. "He wasn't happy, of course, and naturally he was surprised. But he wanted to arrange to see Kwame right away, and I have to tell you, the meeting couldn't have gone any better. Nigel accepted Kwame, but more importantly, Kwame accepted him. In fact, I think he's really excited about the idea of having a dad. His real dad."

"Ah, well, I saw that coming."

Callie frowned. "What do you mean?"

"Kwame always got attached really easily to the guys you were dating. Not that there were a lot of them, but it was clear that he was looking for a father figure. So to find his real father now, I expected no less than for him to accept him wholeheartedly."

Callie thought about her friend's words. Tamara was right. Kwame did get attached easily, which was why she was very careful about not introducing many men into his life. There had been only two, the most recent being a couple years ago, and indeed, Callie had stayed with Philip longer than she normally would have simply because she saw how much Kwame liked him.

"Well, he was even more excited with Nigel than he ever had been with Philip."

"Of course," Tamara said. "Because this time, he's met his real father."

Callie said nothing, her stomach twisting. In a way, this was all so surreal. She and Nigel had reconnected when she had never thought she would ever see him again, and Kwame had fallen for him instantly.

"It's been two days back-to-back that we've gotten together with Nigel," Callie said. She paused before saying, "In fact we're at his house, right now."

"This late?"

"We were watching a movie, and Kwame fell asleep, so Nigel figured it'd be best to just let him sleep… We'll leave in the morning. No big deal."

"No big deal?" Tamara repeated, her tone saying she thought Callie had lost her mind. "You're at Nigel's house at this hour, and Kwame is asleep…heck, why are you talking to me?"

"Nigel's not here," Callie said. "In fact, I wouldn't be surprised if he was off at his girlfriend's place."

"He's got a girlfriend?"

"I…I don't know for sure," Callie admitted, and again she felt a sense of unease at the very idea.

"Well what did he say? Why did he leave you there alone at this hour?"

"He—he didn't say anything. He just left."

"Why?" Tamara asked. "What am I missing?"

Her friend was missing a couple of dots she needed in order to connect the whole picture. "What you're missing," Callie began, then sighed. "Nigel kissed me. He kissed me, and then he left me."

"What?" Tamara shrieked. "You and Nigel—"

"Nigel and I nothing."

"Nothing? You kissed him. You can't call that nothing!"

"What I'm saying is that it didn't mean anything. I think it was just…I don't know. A reaction to the situation."

"Put the two of you within reach of each other, and there are always fireworks."

"Tamara, please."

"Come on, Callie. This is me you're talking to. I went to college with both of you, remember? I knew how much you were in love with Nigel. You think I'm surprised to hear the two of you kissed?"

"And you're already thinking that we're on the road to reconciliation, and I'm trying to make it clear to you that we're not. In fact, I think Nigel was trying to make me feel bad by kissing me." When Tamara scoffed, Callie forged ahead. "He was making it clear to me what I missed out on, not telling me he wanted me back. Seriously, I wouldn't be surprised if he was in another woman's bed right now."

"I would."

Callie ignored the comment. "Look, Nigel was great with how he dealt with me, which I definitely appreciate. He wasn't happy with me for my deception, which was to be expected. But he's welcoming Kwame into his life with open arms, which is the best possible outcome in the situation."

"Sounds like he's doing the same with the mother," Tamara commented.

Callie rolled her eyes. She shouldn't have told her friend about the kiss. That had been a mistake.

Yes, Tamara had known both her and Nigel and had known that their relationship had been hot and intense. But that was a long time ago. "I didn't tell him about his son for ten years. I think it's safe to say that even if he's accepting Kwame, there's no chance of him really wanting to start up a relationship with me again. The kiss was…meaningless. Trust me, he made that clear. Which is fine by me, because I'm not here to rekindle a relationship with Nigel. I know I burned that bridge a long time ago, and I've made my peace with that. In fact, for the longest time I've always thought I would just be a single mother forever. I'll probably be one of those women who meets someone when she's sixty. Once I've raised Kwame and he's out of the house, and I'm satisfied that he's okay, then I'll worry about me."

"That's no fun."

Callie sighed softly. "Tamara, I know you mean well, but I really don't want to talk about me and Nigel. You've got to understand why."

"I do. But what you just told me makes it sound like the

feelings are still there between the two of you. After all you didn't tell me how *you* felt about the kiss—only that it meant nothing to Nigel."

Damn. Tamara was right.

As though she was well aware that she had scored the winning point, Tamara backed down. "I'm glad things are going well. And please tell Nigel I said hi."

"Sure thing," Callie said. "How are you? I didn't ask...."

"I'm okay. Still no sign of Patrick."

"That's both good and bad," Callie said. "Good that he's not harassing you, but bad that he hasn't yet been apprehended. I'll only feel safe when I know he's behind bars."

"Maybe he's actually going to leave me alone."

Callie wouldn't bet on it. "I just hope the police track him down sooner rather than later and you can finally be rid of him."

"Yeah," Tamara said softly, but Callie got the sense that her friend was already having second thoughts about leaving her abusive husband.

It was no surprise why Tamara was all excited about the idea of her and Nigel reconnecting. Tamara was a hopeful romantic. She was married to Patrick, and even though she knew in her heart she was better off without him, Tamara often fell for his crazy excuses and took him back. Callie had a feeling that the abuse in the relationship went far beyond what Tamara had told her about.

This time, however, with the charges against Patrick—including attempted murder for running her and Kwame off the road—Callie hoped he would be a nonissue in Tamara's life from here on out.

"Listen, Callie, I'm gonna get some sleep. But keep me up-to-date, okay?"

"Okay," Callie told her.

And as she ended the call, she glanced at the clock.

Nearly two hours, and still no Nigel.

Chapter 11

"Well, it's good to know you're alive."

Nigel, who had just wandered into the kitchen, met Callie's eyes. He had gone to his favorite bar and chilled with some other cops and Marshall, then crashed at Marshall's place for the remainder of the night. The look on Callie's face said she thought he had spent the night in a brothel.

"I hung out with some cops at a local bar," Nigel said by way of explanation, wondering why he had to explain himself. He had been gone from the house for one night. Callie had been gone for ten years.

Then he went over to Kwame, who sat at the kitchen table with a plate of scrambled eggs and toast in front of him, and put an arm around him from behind. "Morning, son."

Kwame looked up at him, his smile as bright as the sun. "Morning, Dad."

Callie withdrew two coffee mugs from the cupboard. She

placed them on the counter audibly, and Nigel got the sense that she was trying to get his attention.

"I hope you don't mind that I got up and started making breakfast," she said. "We couldn't wait on you forever."

Nigel sauntered over to Callie, suppressing a smile. "Sounds to me like you missed me last night," he couldn't resist saying.

The look she leveled on him was lethal. "I was simply worried that something may have happened to you," she said in a lowered voice.

Or had she spent hours remembering their kiss, as he had?

That was a road Nigel didn't want to go down, even if the heat he'd felt as he had kissed Callie last night was more intense than anything else he'd experienced.

Except, of course, for the last time he'd kissed her....

Not going there, Nigel told himself. So he said something certain to diffuse any sexual tension. "I was gone for one night. You were gone for ten years."

Callie's eyes widened at the comment, then narrowed.

"What?" Nigel went on. "You didn't think I worried about you?"

Callie said nothing, but he could tell by the expression on her face that he'd made his point.

"Mom thought you went to see your girlfriend," Kwame chimed in.

Callie's eyes bulged in mortification. "Kwame!"

"What?" Kwame asked innocently. "When I asked where Dad was, you said you thought he went out to see his girlfriend."

"I—I said *maybe,*" Callie sputtered. She didn't meet Nigel's gaze.

So she cared. That knowledge caused an odd stirring sensation in Nigel's gut.

"Help yourself to coffee, and the rest of the scrambled eggs," Callie told him.

"Aren't you going to eat?" Nigel asked.

"I'm fine with the coffee," she said, her tone clipped. She still didn't meet his gaze.

Oh yeah, she cared. That was clear to Nigel.

"What are we gonna do today, Dad?" Kwame asked.

"You're going to head back home, get showered, spend some time with your aunts," Callie interjected. "I'm sure your father has things to do."

"I've got all day," Nigel said.

"Well I'm sure you…there must be things…I'm sure."

Damn it, watching her sputter, Nigel could feel the sexual tension between them. And he knew that Callie felt it too, which was why she was so hell-bent on getting out of here as soon as possible now that he was here.

He wanted to kiss her again, make it even more clear to her that she'd blown a good thing by leaving.

Or was he really interested in having one more taste of her?

Because certainly he wasn't interested in resuming their relationship. Sexually, his body was reacting to her, but emotionally, he could never trust her with his heart again. Not after what she'd done the first time.

"If Kwame wants to hang with me, it's fine," Nigel said.

"You mean just you and Kwame?"

"Sure. Why not?"

"Oh."

"Please, Mom?"

"I guess…I guess I could go to Uncle Dave's, get freshened up, then come back here with a change of clothes for Kwame."

Kwame leaped from his chair and moments later, was

throwing his arms around his mother's waist. "Thanks, Mom!"

Warmth spread through Nigel.

"All right, then," Callie said. "I'll be back later."

Later was around noon, and only because her sisters had encouraged her to give Kwame time with his father. It had surprisingly been hard to do. Not because she didn't trust Nigel, but because she wanted to be there to see her son through this first phase of getting to know his father.

When she entered the house and followed Nigel into the kitchen, she saw that Kwame was wearing a pair of Nigel's shorts and T-shirt, both too big on him. But there was something endearing about seeing him wearing his father's clothes.

Then Callie noticed the very same thing she had at Uncle Dave's—the house was hot.

"Is the power out here too?" she asked.

Nigel nodded. "Yep."

"That's why we're eating the ice cream," Kwame said. "Before it melts."

Nigel shrugged sheepishly. "Not the best lunch, I know. But we did have turkey sandwiches first."

Callie wasn't about to complain. "Any way to stay cool in this weather. Good Lord, I don't remember it being this hot in Cleveland." Callie was fanning herself with a hand, which was practically pointless.

"The whole neighborhood's without power. The hydro company said it'd be a few hours—at least—before the power comes back on."

"It sucks," Kwame said. "Dad and I went to the store, and he bought a Kinect, and we haven't been able to even try it yet."

"You bought a Kinect?" Callie asked. "He's got a Wii. We could have brought it over here."

"But he doesn't have a Kinect," Nigel said, making it clear that he was going to spoil his son with gifts.

He was entitled, wasn't he?

"Gosh, I could use a bowl of that ice cream," Callie said. "What a day to lose power. They say it's going to be a scorcher."

"You should be used to this in Florida," Nigel said.

"With air conditioning," Callie stressed. "We couldn't survive in Florida without AC."

For the end of May, this weather was bizarre. Callie was used to hot days in Florida, but the heat here in Cleveland was just as intense, and it was much farther north.

Kwame, who had just eaten a bowl of ice cream, slumped forward, looking miserable. "I'm hot."

"I know, baby. But you won't be hot for long, because guess what?"

"What?" Kwame asked.

"One of Uncle Dave's nephews is having a birthday party today. He's turning six, and he's going to a big indoor play place. I know you might think you're a bit too old for that, but I'm sure it will be air-conditioned, and you'll be able to cool off. And it will be a way for you to get to know some of the other kids in the family. What do you think?"

"But I was having fun with Dad."

"And you'll see him as soon as the party is over," Callie pointed out. "This is a great time to get to know some of the family you've never met."

"Your mother's right," Nigel said. "And hopefully, once the party is over, the power will be back on around here."

Kwame shrugged. "Okay."

Callie couldn't help thinking about what Tamara had said, that Kwame was extra attached to Nigel because he had finally met his real father. Clearly Tamara was right, because Callie had never known her son to say no to a birthday party.

Callie looked toward Nigel. "The party's at two. If you're not free to take us, I'll call a tax—"

"I'll take you."

Callie wasn't sure if Nigel's voice sounded a little annoyed, as though she should know that he would take her, but she didn't want to expect things of him. "Thank you," she said. "I think this will offer the perfect solution for Kwame to get out of the heat. And then you can come back here and spend more time with your dad." Callie looked toward Kwame who seemed content with the plan.

They didn't last more than another thirty minutes in the house. It was simply too hot. So Nigel headed to a Best Buy and allowed Kwame to shop for as many movies as he wanted.

"You don't have to spoil him," Callie had said.

"I haven't been able to buy him anything in nine years. This is hardly spoiling."

Callie had put up her hands, knowing this was an argument she couldn't win.

A dozen DVDs later—and a couple more games for the Kinect—they were finally en route to the birthday party. It took about fifteen minutes to get to the establishment where the party was being held.

It looked too small to house any sort of play place. But once Callie went inside with Kwame, she saw that looks were indeed deceiving. There were climbing structures and bouncy castles and slides—a total funland for kids. Children were screaming happily as they were climbing, jumping and running around to their heart's content.

"Are you going to stick around?" Nigel asked.

Hiding her shock, Callie turned around to face him. She didn't even know he had exited the car, and certainly hadn't heard him come up behind her.

"I can, I guess." She shrugged.

"If it's all right with you, I wouldn't mind if you came back to the house with me. I know it's hot but…but I figured this might be a good time to talk."

Maybe that was exactly what they needed, to talk. Because after that kiss last night, today had been awkward to say the least. They had been walking on tiptoes around each other, and clearly Nigel wanted to resolve some things. Perhaps set up some boundaries.

She nodded. "Just let me get Kwame into the party, and I'll head off with you then."

Several minutes later, after meeting Uncle Dave's side of the family and saying hello and promising to be back within two hours, Callie left the building and climbed into Nigel's black Buick LeSabre.

They drove in silence for a while, the only sounds in the car that of the radio station, which was currently playing an old-school mix. It was the kind of music that brought Callie right back to when she had been dating Nigel, which was something she knew she was better off forgetting.

After a while, Callie said, "I wonder if I should have stayed there with him. He doesn't really know anyone."

"He'll be fine," Nigel said. "This will give him a chance to get to know the extended family. There are kids close to his age, so that's great. And the party's only going on for a couple of hours."

Callie nodded, knowing it was true. She wasn't against Kwame spending time with Uncle Dave's side of the family. What really bothered her was the fact that she would now be alone with Nigel.

The moment they were alone last night, she had felt uneasy—and with good reason. Because he had ultimately kissed her.

Which had only clouded the issue—and the issue was that

they were supposed to become friends again in order to better parent Kwame.

Callie sensed Nigel's eyes on her and looked in his direction. And darn it, just one glance at him had her heart beating out of control.

She jerked her gaze away, and instead looked out the passenger window. Clearly, it would take some getting used to Nigel being in her life again. Her body had to forget all the pleasure he had given her as a lover, because now they were going to be just friends.

Callie glanced at Nigel again, noticed the firm set of his jaw. Something was bothering him. Her heart deflated. How silly she had been to be thinking of the kiss, because it was suddenly obvious that he didn't have anything amorous on his mind.

He was still upset with her. She got the sense that he was going to give her a piece of his mind about her deception.

Callie swallowed. She had resolved to let Nigel express any feelings he had, unsavory or not. She deserved to deal with whatever he had to say.

But Nigel stayed silent. And no sooner than he pulled onto the highway, the sky opened up and the rain started to come down.

"Well, I saw that coming," he commented as he peered upward through the windshield. "With the incredible heat, these sudden downpours are to be expected. The earth is simply too hot, and the rain has to cool it down."

So they were going to talk about the weather. "That's Miami in the summer," Callie said softly. "There's a shower practically every day. But I love the rain. Like you said, it cools things down, so that's always nice."

"You like it in Miami?" Nigel asked.

"I love it. The first year I went there, it was so nice to not have to live through winter. Something as simple as not being weighted down by a heavy coat is more liberating than you can imagine. I'm not sure I could get used to winter in the north again. I've been so spoiled."

"Hmm."

At the sound, Callie looked at Nigel. And frowned. She suddenly got the sense that he had asked her that question for another reason—to gauge if she would be willing to move back to Cleveland.

He wouldn't really ask her to do that, would he? It was something she hadn't even considered. Uproot her son and herself?

"Listen," Callie began. "I know things are…tense between us…and I also know that it's my fault. But I hope there's a way that you and I can work things out."

Nigel's head turned toward hers, the look of shock on his face palpable. "Pardon me?"

"That's not what I meant," Callie quickly said, realizing how her words had been construed. "We have a son, and here we are spending time together, but you barely want to look at me. You kissed me last night, and then you took off. Clearly, there's a lot of unresolved anger, and I totally get it. But what I really want is for us to get past that. For Kwame's sake, if not our own."

"How about telling me what's really going on with you?"

That wasn't what Callie had expected to hear. "What do you mean?"

"You think I don't remember you?" Nigel asked, his voice now an octave lower. "Remember how you looked when you were stressed? And as much as this situation is, as you say, tense, I get the feeling something else is going on with you."

Was he really that intuitive? She remembered how he had been able to easily gauge her moods in the past, but that had been a long time ago.

"So?" Nigel prompted.

"I learned something," she found herself saying. "About my mother."

Nigel's eyebrows rose. "You know what happened to her?"

Callie shook her head. "No. But I learned that she was apparently in some kind of trouble. My aunt left a letter for me and my sisters. She said that my mother left us with her because she wanted to protect us. That was all."

Nigel frowned. "She had no idea what the trouble was?"

"No. Not really. But she suspected it had to do with an ex-boyfriend, perhaps. Or something involving the law." Callie shrugged. "She also said that my mother was ashamed to come back into our lives. Something about her having not made the best choices before."

"Hmm." Nigel was no longer looking at her, but at the road. Callie couldn't help wondering if he was thinking about the choice *she* had made.

"And what else?" Nigel asked. "Because that story about your head and arm? You said it was a fender bender, but it was more serious than that. And Kwame said something about you being followed by someone on the road?"

Callie swallowed. Kwame had told him that?

"You can talk to me, Callie. We might not be in a relationship anymore, but you can still tell me anything."

Hearing Nigel say that, Callie felt a wave of emotion. He could so easily not care about her personal dilemmas, but he was being the same caring man she had known him to be.

"You're right. There is something else." She closed her eyes a moment before continuing. "It has to do with a friend of mine. A friend whose husband has been acting like a royal jerk. He's abusive, and there are criminal charges against him, but Patrick was out on bail. Which is insane, if you ask me. You let a ticking time bomb out of jail? Well, he was angry because I helped my friend leave him. So angry that he came after me."

"Are you telling me he deliberately ran you off the road?" Nigel asked, suddenly sounding more serious.

"I don't know if that was Patrick's intention, but yes, I noticed him following me. I tried to avoid him, but I couldn't. He wouldn't get off my tail. And the next thing I knew, he was bumping into my car and I was veering off the road."

"You could have been killed," Nigel said, his jaw clenched.

Callie nodded. Though she didn't want to accept that grim fact, she knew that it was true. "I'm grateful Kwame wasn't hurt."

"But you were."

"I'll survive."

A beat passed. "So this guy's bond was revoked, right? He's behind bars."

"Actually, no."

"What?"

"He's alluded the law. And yes, I'm worried about it. He's really angry that my friend left him. Unstable. Given how irrational he is, I was kind of figuring that until he's caught, I should stay in Cleveland."

Nigel was silent a moment. Then he said, "Tell me something. If not for this Patrick guy being on the lamb, would you even be here? Or would you have returned home already?"

"I…I don't know," Callie answered honestly.

Nigel's jaw tightened. "I see."

"I'm not saying I wouldn't have told you about Kwame. That I wouldn't stick around longer for you to spend time with him. It's just…naturally, until the police apprehend Patrick, how can I really feel safe?"

Alicia Keys's "Fallin'" began to play on the radio, and Callie's breath oozed out of her. Slowly, she looked at Nigel. He was staring at her, the same shock she was feeling evident on his face.

This had been their song ten years ago.

Suddenly, Callie was remembering the amount of times she and Nigel had gotten naked to this song and made sweet love. And she couldn't help wondering if Nigel was thinking the same thing, too.

He looked away, breaking their eye contact, and turned the radio off. Then he said, "Ironic, isn't it?"

"What's ironic?" Callie asked, a mix of emotions swirling through her. Alicia Keys's smooth voice may not have been filling the car anymore, but Callie had already been transported back in time.

"Once, you hated cops," Nigel said. "Hated them so much you broke up with me when I decided to join the force. Now, in order for your life to get back on track, you need the police."

"I'm ten years older, Nigel. You don't have to rub in my face how immature I once was. You asked me what was going on, so I told you. But forget I said anything."

"It's so simple for you, isn't it? You left me, you lied to me, but hey, you were immature. That makes it all okay."

"That's not what I said."

"What I want to know is when you matured. Two years after you left me? Five years?"

Callie was surprised to see Nigel turning into his driveway. She hadn't even noticed that they'd entered his neighborhood. "What's your point?"

Nigel turned off the car. "Ten years?"

"What's your point?" Callie repeated.

"If you *matured* years ago, why wouldn't you tell me about Kwame then?"

"Fine. I'm still immature. Still a hot mess. Okay?" There was no point explaining anything to Nigel. It was clear that not only would he never forgive her, he would use every opportunity to tell her how wrong she'd been.

She opened the car door and jumped out. She didn't need

this. The rain immediately drenched her, but that didn't stop her from heading in the direction of the road that didn't lead to Nigel's front door.

"Callie, where are you going?" Nigel called.

She didn't answer, just started to run on the sidewalk.

"Callie."

Callie picked up speed, not caring that the rain was coming down in sheets. She could hardly see and the heavy drops were splashing her face. But she didn't stop.

"Callie!" Nigel called, more urgent this time.

But she didn't stop.

Was he going to be mad at her forever? She understood that she'd made a mistake, but was he so perfect? He was acting as though he'd never done anything wrong in his life.

When he'd accused her of sleeping with Jeremiah, Callie had been crushed.

It wasn't that she hadn't matured over the years. But she'd been in too deep.

Tears fell, mixing with the rain. This was too hard. It hurt too much to be around Nigel knowing that he would be forever angry at her. She wished she could just put armor around her heart and not feel any pain. But the disapproval from a man she had once loved so wholeheartedly was hard to bear.

"Callie!" He was closer.

She kept going, wanting to put as much distance between them as possible, aware that she was accomplishing nothing, except getting soaked. But his disappointment, on the heels of her feeling that they'd made some headway, was especially hurtful.

And that damn Alicia Keys song. Callie had so badly wanted him to take her in his arms....

She gasped when she felt the strong hand wrap around her upper arm. A moment later, she was being whirled around.

"What are you doing?" Nigel asked. The rain pounded his skin.

"You hate me. I get it."

"Hate you?" Nigel's eyes bulged, as if the mere suggestion was the most ludicrous thing on the earth.

"Yes, hate me. I know I hurt you, and if I could take it back, I would." Her voice cracked. "I—I would."

"Damn it, woman," Nigel uttered. "I don't hate you."

And then he pulled her against his chest.

And right there in the rain, he brought his mouth down on hers.

Hard.

Chapter 12

Callie's first reaction was utter disbelief. She couldn't believe what was happening.

But it took only a few seconds for the reality of the situation to register in her brain.

Nigel Williams was kissing her.

And not the same kind of kiss like last night, one designed to make it clear what she'd left behind. But one that was full of heat and need.

Callie felt his chest rumble against her body, and good Lord, what an erotic charge! Despite the coolness of the rain, heat spread through her body.

And no longer was she questioning why Nigel was kissing her, but rather allowing herself to feel. Feel what she had not experienced in ten years.

Emotion came bubbling forward in a way that startled her. Intense desire mixed with warmth and affection. Certainly she shouldn't still feel something for Nigel.

But as his lips moved over hers, she knew otherwise.

With a gasp, she opened her mouth wider for him. And as her good hand snaked around Nigel's strong back, she forgot all about the fact that they were still standing in the rain. Two people furiously kissing each other as the rain poured down.

It was a thunderous boom that had both of them springing apart, though the boom could have easily come from inside Callie—that's how stimulated she was right now. She was hot and bothered and remembering just how good she and Nigel had been together.

Her chest heaved with ragged breaths as she stared up at him. He gazed down at her. For a long moment, even though the rain seemed to be coming down harder, neither moved. Neither said a word.

Nigel was the one to break the silence. "I don't hate you."

Callie said nothing. She was still reeling from the kiss.

Nigel put his arm around her shoulder, pulled her close. He began to walk with her. "Come on. Let's get inside the house."

Once they were in the foyer, and Callie realized just how completely soaked to the bone she was, she felt stupid. Until Nigel turned to her and touched the hem of her shirt, saying, "We need to get you out of these clothes."

And just like that, her body was buzzing. She knew he was right—clearly she would need to take off her wet clothes. But hearing him speak the idea of undressing her…well, it turned her on.

Nigel took her hand. "Come this way."

He led her across the mahogany floors, which Callie knew he had painstakingly refinished himself. She hoped they wouldn't be ruined.

But she stopped thinking about the floors the moment she

entered the laundry room and saw Nigel pull his wet T-shirt over his head. He plopped it into the laundry sink.

And the sight of that hard body of his, all perfect muscles except for that scar…Callie lost her breath.

"Put your clothes in the sink," Nigel said. "I'll wash them, put them in the dryer."

Nodding, Callie began to try to maneuver out of her sling, but it was harder than normal. Either because she was wet, or because she was nervous.

And then Nigel slipped out of his jeans, and Callie gulped when she saw him in his boxers, which were clinging to his body. Goodness, she had thought he was fine years ago, but his body was even more magnificent now. His legs were thicker, stronger. He had morphed into a fully-fledged man.

"Let me help you," Nigel said, and approached her.

Then, gingerly, he helped undo the sling and guide her arm out. Callie didn't speak as he then began to pull the wet shirt over her body. He tossed it into the sink.

"How does your arm feel?" he asked.

Callie was feeling no pain. None at all. "It's fine."

"Your jeans will be difficult to get off. I'll do it."

And when he undid the button, Callie's center began to pulse wildly. Nigel was taking her clothes off….

His strong hands moved down her thighs as he helped her out of her jeans, and Callie thought she would die from the lust coursing through her body.

As he pulled the second jean leg off of her body, he looked up at her. Met her gaze.

Callie swallowed. She was wearing only her underwear and bra, and wanted nothing more than for Nigel to touch and kiss every inch of her body.

He didn't move. And she just knew that he was thinking the same thing she was…that they should shed the rest of their clothes and get on with it.

"It wasn't easy for me," Callie said, not sure why she felt compelled to say that at this of all moments. "Leaving. I just want you to know that."

And then Nigel ran both of his palms up the back of her legs, setting her skin on fire. "Did you miss this?" he asked, his voice low, deep. "Did you miss me touching you like this?"

Callie drew in a shuddery breath. "Yes. Oh, yes."

Nigel pressed his lips to her belly, and tentacles of pleasure exploded all through Callie's body. Slowly rising, he kissed a path up her torso, through the valley between her breasts, stopping when he got to the underside of her neck.

"How could you do it?" he asked.

Surprised at the question, Callie looked at him. His eyes were heated, his breathing ragged. All she could say was, "I'm sorry, Nigel."

"What exactly are you sorry for?" Nigel asked, a challenge in his voice.

"I'm sorry that I was immature." *Please don't stop touching me now....* "I'm sorry that I left you and never told you I was pregnant."

"And that's all?"

"Isn't that enough?"

Nigel slipped his hands into her hair and lowered his face close to hers. "No. No, it's not enough. I don't want to hear that you're sorry because you left, simply because you think you didn't do right by me in terms of keeping our son a secret. I want to hear that you regret what you did because you destroyed *us.* Because we had something good, Callie. We had something good and you threw it away."

Callie's heart stopped. She saw the fury in Nigel's eyes, but in his touch she felt passion. Because the way he was tipping her head backward, forcing her mouth to angle upward to his, made it clear he wanted to kiss her again.

Her lips parted as he continued to stare at her, and she

thought about what she had not allowed herself to think about for ten years. That yes, she had thrown away the best thing that would ever come into her life by leaving Nigel.

"You think I don't remember just how good we were to-gether?" she asked, her chest shuddering. "You think I forgot everything?"

Nigel stared down at Callie. At her parted lips and the desire pooling in her eyes. She hadn't exactly answered his question, but it was enough. It was enough because the hor-mones raging through Nigel's body were overpowering him. He couldn't stand being this close to her and not acting on what he was feeling. So he snaked one arm around her waist and pulled her moist body against his. And then, God help him, he couldn't hold back any longer.

He brought his mouth down on hers, needing to feel her surrender to him once more. She moaned immediately, a soft and sweet sound, and then she opened her mouth for him, as though there was nothing in the world she wanted to do more than this.

And there was nothing more Nigel wanted. Oh, he'd told himself that he *didn't* want her, that he despised her even, but it was all a lie. Because the only thing that mattered to him was holding Callie in his arms.

It was the only thing that had ever mattered.

"I missed this." Nigel's mouth moved from her lips to the underside of her jaw, and he was rewarded when she dug her fingers into his shoulders and trembled against him. "And I can tell that you missed it, too."

"Yes," Callie rasped. "No one has compared to you…. No one…."

She may as well have told him to give it to her right here in the laundry room, that's how powerful a reaction he had to her words.

But those same words made him think of something else. There were ten years between them, and God only knew how many other boyfriends. Nigel hated the very knowledge that another man had ever touched her this way.

He drew her earlobe between his teeth, and tightened his arms around her as she moaned. He didn't want to think about anyone else, anything else, but them.

But he did want to set her mind at ease, in case she had any doubts. "So you know," he whispered in her ear, "what you said to Kwame, it isn't true. I don't have a girlfriend. I've been single for a good year and a half."

Callie looked up at him from heavy-lidded eyes. And despite her obvious lust, she grinned. "That's when I broke up with my last boyfriend. A year and a half ago."

"Good. Because that means there's no reason for us not to continue…" He twirled his tongue beneath her earlobe. "…this." Not that it would matter if Callie told him she was dating someone else, because the way she was mewling and responding to his every touch, Nigel saw her the same as he did ten years ago.

As his.

Surely an experience as explosive as what they had shared together, as meaningful, couldn't so easily be shared with someone else with the same intensity.

Callie stroked his face, and Nigel's mouth went back to hers. He kissed her deeply, and Callie reciprocated with fervor. Her tongue tangled with his, and he tugged gently on her hair while his other hand covered her bra. He pushed the wet fabric out of the way and stroked her nipple with his fingers, and groaned with pleasure when it hardened against his hand.

"Yes, Callie. I know exactly what this is doing to you. Because I never forgot. All these years, I never forgot."

Callie arched her back, but Nigel drew her face to his and

ravaged her mouth. Callie dragged her fingernails down the skin of his back, then broke the kiss and stared at him, a grin tugging at the corner of her mouth.

"So you remember, too," he said.

"How could I forget?"

And then Callie moved forward, slipping her hands beneath the waist of his boxers. She tugged at them, then said, "Ouch."

Nigel looked at her in concern. "Your arm?"

"I'm okay. I just need to take it easier."

"You're sure?"

She placed her uninjured hand over his throbbing erection. "I'm sure."

Nigel scooped her into his arms. He kissed her as he carried her to his bedroom. Once there, he set her on her feet and then moved his mouth to her earlobe again and felt a rush of excitement when she quivered.

Then his hands went to her bra. He fought with the wet, uncooperative material as if it were his enemy, needing to get it off of her body in a hurry. And when she was topless, he kissed her again—a soft, deep kiss that was all about emotion.

"Make love to me," Callie pleaded.

Nigel needed no further encouragement. He slipped his boxers off and kicked them aside. Then he went to Callie and dragged her underwear over her hips.

His eyes drank in the beautiful sight of her nakedness, a body that was more curvy than before. Breasts that were larger.

Somehow, she was even sexier than she had been years ago. And his desire for her was greater than he had ever known.

Taking her hand, he led her to the bed. He sat, then urged her onto him. She put her legs on either side of him, and Nigel growled with pleasure.

Her breasts were eye level to his face, and he drew one nipple into his mouth. The skin puckered and hardened as his tongue twirled over it, and Callie moaned.

"Yes, baby," Nigel said, and moved his mouth to her other breast. With his fingers, he played with her other nipple, and took pleasure in the sounds of her deep sighs.

Reaching for her head, he drew her face to his and kissed her. Kissed her as he eased onto his back. And as their tongues mated, Nigel guided his erection into her sweet, soft place.

Callie gasped. "Nigel..."

"Yes, baby." He placed his hands on her hips, guiding her against him to match his movements. She held her injured arm close to her body, but her other arm was already moving upward, her fingers sliding through her wet hair. Her eyes were closed, the expression of erotic bliss heightening his own desire.

He picked up speed, and Callie did as well, her sounds of rapture growing louder.

"Yes," Nigel said, as they found their old rhythm. She was a vision of loveliness. "Oh, Callie..."

She opened her eyes. Looked down at him. He covered both of her nipples as he thrust upward and deep inside of her.

Callie cried out in pleasure. "Nigel, I'm already close."

"Kiss me."

She dropped her body downward onto his, her mouth finding his. His tongue tangling with hers, he thrust deeper. She sighed into his mouth, and Nigel wrapped both of his arms around her waist and didn't relent in his kissing as his speed of lovemaking went into overdrive. And soon, Callie was tearing her mouth from his and crying out in pleasure as her body quivered against him.

"Oh, Nigel. Oh, baby!"

As she succumbed to her release, Nigel gave in to his orgasm.

And was all too aware that he'd just given Callie back a piece of his heart.

Callie and Nigel didn't have much time after making love to get ready to get Kwame. In fact, Callie's clothes were all still wet, because neither she nor Nigel had put them in the dryer before they'd ended up in the bedroom. They hadn't even stopped to check if the power had come back on.

It had—which they'd discovered once they'd realized they couldn't spend the entire afternoon in bed if they were going to get Kwame in time. Which left Callie with a quandary. Either head back to the birthday party wearing Nigel's clothes, or stay at his house and wait for her clothes to dry.

Callie opted to wait for her clothes to dry. She didn't want to confuse Kwame by showing up wearing Nigel's clothes.

He was gone now, and since Callie was down from her sexual high, she felt awkward. Because she had just made love to the man she had once been crazy about. And she didn't even know if he liked her anymore, much less loved her.

Had they simply gotten caught up in the emotions of the situation? She'd been crying and in distress and Nigel had reacted as he always had in the past, trying to comfort her.

That comforting had led them to the bedroom.

But good Lord, what an experience! Callie didn't remember their lovemaking ever being so hot and frenzied. But perhaps it had, and she had simply forgotten. Whatever the case, sleeping with Nigel had proven to her once again just how great they were together in bed.

But what next?

Had they simply scratched an itch, satisfied their curiosity? Because Lord knew, they'd always connected in an amazing way between the sheets.

Callie wasn't sure what to think. She only knew that things had changed in a way she hadn't expected.

But had they changed for the better, or for the worse?

Chapter 13

Two more days passed with Callie and Kwame spending much of their time with Nigel. Two more days in which Callie felt more and more awkward.

Ever since Nigel had returned home with Kwame after the birthday party, they hadn't spent a moment alone together. She and Nigel hadn't really talked. Not about what had happened between them, in any case. And Nigel certainly hadn't interacted with her like a man who'd taken her to the heights of pleasure in his bedroom.

In fact, he was back to being somewhat closed off. He had made sweet love to her—and then it was back to business as usual.

Which only had Callie feeling angry with herself for hoping that it would have been any other way. She hadn't come back to reconcile with him, but that one sweet taste of him had caused her priorities to get screwed up.

This morning, Callie had dropped off Kwame and then

left. Nigel said he wanted to take Kwame to the police station. Callie went back to her uncle's place to spend some time with her sisters. They'd spent hours shopping and talking about how they could go about finding out about their mother's past. Callie knew she could ask Nigel, but didn't feel right about asking him for anything. Especially not now. She still remembered his comment about irony. She had once hated cops, but now needed them in order to feel like she could get on with her life.

It was shortly after four when she got to Nigel's house. She knocked, but got no answer, so she tried the door and found it unlocked. Inside, she heard no sound, and headed downstairs, figuring Kwame and Nigel were perhaps in the home theater. But once she got to the basement, it was even quieter.

So she went back upstairs and wandered into the kitchen. And that was when she spotted them through the back window. They were sitting at the patio table, talking.

Callie stopped in her tracks, struck by just how sweet this moment was. Father and son, together, having a simple conversation.

She could see the joy in her son's eyes, even from her vantage point. And it was this joy that had her biting her tongue every time she thought she would suggest he spend more time with other family members, not just his father.

Kwame turned, saw her. And then he jumped up from his chair and ran to the patio door.

Callie met him as he was opening it. "Hey, you."

"I had an awesome time at the police station!" Kwame exclaimed.

Callie met Nigel's gaze. He looked at her briefly, then glanced away. "Is that so?"

"Dad even took me for a ride in a police car."

"Sounds like you had an awesome day."

"I did."

Callie was still hugging her son when she noticed movement at the side of the yard. And then a young boy came into view.

"Nathan!" Kwame exclaimed, releasing her and running down the deck's steps.

"Who's that?" Callie asked.

"My neighbor. He's an only child. Once he learned Kwame was my son, he was very happy. He's got someone to play with."

Nathan was holding a soccer ball, which he promptly dropped, and he and Kwame began to kick it. Callie stood and silently watched, crossing her arms over her chest.

"I think this is a good time to talk," Nigel said, finally speaking to her.

Callie looked at him, her pulse speeding up. "Sure."

Nigel gestured to a chair. "Sit."

Callie could only imagine that he finally wanted to talk to her about what had happened between them. "What's on your mind?"

"I was thinking that you and Kwame should move in with me."

Callie's eyes bulged. "What?"

"You should move in with me."

"But—but what about your job?"

"What about it?"

Move in with him? Callie's breath was suddenly coming in harsh spurts. Because she was thinking of spending nights in Nigel's bed once Kwame was asleep…. "There's no need to move in with you. We've been here every day. We can schedule our lives around you, be around when you need us."

"I need you around all the time."

Callie shuddered at the words, her mind suddenly venturing to something else, thinking of a deeper meaning behind what he'd said. She knew, however, that Nigel was not speaking about anything that would involve her and him.

Because if he was, he would have shown some sign of affection toward her in the last two days. Instead, he seemed to be avoiding her.

"We're close by, Nigel. We can come over any time. And you're probably returning to work any day now…"

"I've taken extended time off of work. I had vacation coming anyway, but I've got some flexibility because of my position, seniority and the fact that I pretty much don't ever take a vacation. So I booked several weeks off. I would very much like to have Kwame living with me, because…well, because I'd really like that. And obviously, I'm figuring you would want to be here, as well. In fact, being able to give him two parents might be nice."

Callie closed her eyes briefly. Oh yes, she knew that would be Kwame's dream—a home with two parents. "So you want me to move in with you?" Hearing herself, she quickly corrected her words. "I mean, me and Kwame."

"I have missed out on nine years of his life. I can't see any better way to get to know him than to live with him day in, day out. We can be like a family. I think it will be good for him."

But what about for me? was the thought that popped into Callie's mind. How good would this be for her?

She wanted to ask him about them, to at least get an idea of what he was feeling. If he thought that having sex with her was a mistake that should never happen again, shouldn't he just say so?

But with Kwame and his new friend playing not even fifty feet away, this wasn't the right time to broach the subject. So she said, "How about I think about it, get back to you?"

"It would mean a lot to me," Nigel said, his voice holding

a note of something Callie hadn't heard in a long time. A hint of vulnerability? It tugged at her heartstrings.

"All right," she finally said. "I see your point, and I agree—it'll be good for Kwame. We'll move in with you. But it'll be tomorrow, okay? Because my sisters want to take Kwame out tonight."

"Sounds great. You can get your belongings together, and I can come pick you up."

He made it all sound so easy, which she supposed it was when your heart wasn't on the line. He had made love to her, but it had simply been about comfort and familiarity, and perhaps a biological need to get laid.

Yet for her…

For me, nothing, Callie told herself. She had fallen into Nigel's bed, a familiar and exciting place. But that was all. She wasn't naive enough to forget that they hadn't been getting along when she had left him. No, she shouldn't have deceived him about their son, but it wasn't as though she'd run out on him when he had been a perfect partner.

But they could live together. No big deal.

"And hey," Nigel began, leaning forward and speaking in a quieter tone, "what happened between us—let's not read anything into that. It just…happened. I'm willing to move beyond it if you are."

Callie's heart plummeted, though she didn't know why. She had thought the very same thing, hadn't she? That they'd had sex, but it didn't mean anything. Yet hearing Nigel say the words left her feeling slightly unsettled. "Sure. I can move beyond it."

"I think it's best. If we're going to be living together. We don't want to cloud the issue."

"Right. Of course." And for good measure, Callie forced a smile.

No more hot sex. She could handle that.

But a voice in Callie's head called her a big fat liar.

Later that night, after a trip to a laser gaming establishment where Kwame, Callie and his aunts played to their heart's content, Callie broke the news to her son that they would be moving in with his father.

Kwame had no reservations at all. In fact, he was far more excited than Callie had known him to be before. "Nothing's really changing," Callie said. "We'll just be spending more time with your dad."

"But this will be better, because now we'll be a family."

Callie looked at her son and smiled softly. Then she stroked his cheek. "Kwame, I think it's important for you to remember that your father and I have not been together for ten years. He's getting to know you, which is great. But we're not going to be a family—not in the sense of a mom and dad who love each other." She wanted to make sure that he understood that. "We are, however, getting along, which is great. You and Nigel will always be family. He'll always be your father. And because I'm your mother, I am also forever connected to Nigel. We want to be the best parents we can be to you, which is why we're going to live together for a while. But it's not about being a *real* family. Understand?"

Kwame nodded. But Callie got the sense that he wasn't pleased by her words. He was hoping for the whole fairy tale. A father and a mother who were in love—the kind of family life that he had never gotten to experience.

Callie leaned forward and kissed her son on the temple. She understood why he was hopeful. What child didn't want to see his parents together? Even if that child had not known his father for the first nine years of his life, it completely made sense that Kwame wanted the instant family—the kind of family most of his friends at school had.

Kids didn't like to feel different, and Kwame was no exception.

Her son's disappointment also made Callie feel a tiny bit sad for the fact that she couldn't be the be-all and end-all for him. She had tried to be both mother and father, and had done a pretty good job balancing both roles. But she still wasn't a substitute for both a mother and a father.

"You and Dad were in love once," Kwame said, his expression hopeful. "Maybe you can be again."

Callie opened her mouth to protest, but thought better of it. She didn't have to burst her son's bubble of hope.

Not yet.

"What?" Marshall said, staring at Nigel as if he'd grown a second head.

Nigel had gone in to the station to do a little research and tie up some loose ends, and after learning that Big Boy— Jaleel Thompson—had been apprehended for the murder last week, he had told Marshall about his plans to have Callie move in with him.

"You heard me," Nigel said.

"You've got to be careful, man," Marshall said. "I like Callie, but she ran off the first time. She's got a life in Miami now. Who's to say she won't take off again?"

"For one thing, I know about Kwame now. There's no reason for her to run off again. Besides, this time around we're not involved romantically." Nigel's jaw tightened as he thought of that hot afternoon they'd spent making love. Something Nigel had regretted afterward. Not so much regretted, because he had enjoyed the experience, but he'd had to remind himself that letting his guard down with Callie again would be a foolish thing to do.

Besides not being certain he could totally forgive her deception, there was another big concern. She had yet to talk to him—really talk to him—about why she'd left. Nigel had his own suspicions, and knew that her mother abandoning her had affected her in a negative way. If Callie hadn't gotten over her personal demons, she would never truly be free to give her heart completely.

"But you two are playing house," Marshall said. "And I know you—you always burned a torch for her. And your ex Angie—she didn't stand a chance with you because your heart was still with Callie. So I think that it's likely you might start having some real feelings for her again."

"What should I do?" Nigel asked, a hint of exasperation in his tone. "Pretend that I don't have a son? Send her back to Miami? I've got to do what I'm doing. I'm making the best of a tough situation."

"I'm just saying, be careful. You know, try to keep your heart out of it this time."

"You really ought to give me more credit than that," Nigel said as he logged off of his computer. "I'm the one who dealt with losing Callie. I'm very well aware of the fact that she ran the first chance she could. So if you think I'm going to let myself fall for her again, you're out of your mind. What I'm doing right now is getting to know my son. Because like it or not, I have a child with her."

Marshall suddenly gave him an odd look. "Wait a minute. Have you and Callie…" His eyes narrowed.

Nigel rose. "I'm leaving."

"Oh, man. You have, haven't you? I know you, remember? And I can tell you're keeping something from me."

"Goodbye," Nigel said. And then he wiggled his fingers over his shoulders, not daring to look back.

Chapter 14

"Hey, Mom. Come see what Dad's doing!"

Callie had been in a deep sleep, but her son's excited voice woke her with the effectiveness of a bullhorn. She got off of the bed and slipped on the robe that was hanging behind the door.

She made her way to living room, and not seeing Nigel nor Kwame there, she then went to the kitchen. But they weren't there, either.

Turning, her gaze wandered to the large window in the dining room area, where she finally saw Kwame on the deck. He was outside in his pajamas.

Callie made her way to the backyard deck, where she looked over the railing and saw Nigel with a large blue tarp on the ground.

"What are you doing?" she asked.

"It's been a hot summer so far," Nigel said. "I figured Kwame needs a pool."

"You bought him a pool?"

"Yep."

"I can't believe it. My own pool!" Kwame bounded down the steps onto the grass.

Callie followed her son, walking slowly down the steps. She surveyed the array of boxes on the ground and the pile of white steel poles. This was clearly one of those pools that people put up with metal frames. At least those looked sturdier than the giant blow-up ones.

From the shape of the tarp Nigel had spread out on the ground, Callie could tell that it was a rectangular pool, and one that appeared pretty large.

There was also a giant hose, and what must have been a filter. Even if Callie had had her morning cup of coffee, she knew she wouldn't make one lick of sense of it.

"How much did this cost?" It had to be one of the more expensive ones.

"Did you see Kwame's face? Priceless."

"Okay, I understand," she acknowledged. "Don't you need some help to put this up?"

"Nope. I've got it."

But an hour later, Nigel was still wrestling with getting the pool base just right, so Callie went back outside to offer him help. She smirked when he all but grunted that he could handle this himself.

He was one of those guys, the type who believed in doing everything on their own. Mr. Fix-It, Mr. Handyman—the kind who never liked to concede defeat.

"Are you at least ready for some breakfast? Say the word and I'll start your pancakes."

It took Nigel another hour—and two tall glasses of lemonade—before he was ready for a break. Callie served him up a full plate of pancakes, as well as turkey bacon—the kind of breakfast that would give him more energy to get back to the work of putting up the pool.

It took the better part of the day for Nigel to erect a low wood frame to level off the ground, before he installed the pool unit. Once he got to connecting the metal poles, things went more smoothly. Kwame helped as much as he could, and they were all relieved when the pool was ready to be filled with water.

It was certainly big enough to give all of them room to frolic around on a hot day and stay cool. And Kwame could not have looked more excited.

"Here," Callie said, placing a plate of fried chicken, rice and green beans onto the patio table in front of Nigel. "You've put in a full day's work. You really deserve a decent meal."

"Thanks." But Nigel didn't touch the plate of food first, instead he drank half the contents of the tall glass of water.

"Let me get you something else," Callie said. She disappeared inside, then returned with a bottle of beer. "Feel free to start eating. I'll bring out Kwame's and mine in a few minutes."

"No, I'll wait for you," Nigel said. "You didn't have to wait for me to eat, so the least I can do is wait for you to join me."

"You did all the hard work."

"We'll eat as a family," Nigel said.

Minutes later, Callie was heading back outside with plates of food for her and Kwame. "Kwame," she called to her son, who was down by the pool, watching it fill with water. "Come on up for dinner."

As Kwame started across the yard and toward the deck, Callie said to Nigel, "I appreciate you getting the pool. I appreciate you going to this trouble for Kwame."

"He's my son. I'm happy to do this."

"All the same, I appreciate it."

"This is gonna be awesome, Dad!" Kwame announced as he joined them at the table.

"Kwame, why don't you say grace?" Callie suggested.

He folded his hands in front of his face and closed his eyes, and Callie did the same. "Dear God," Kwame began, "thank You for this food we are about to eat. And thank You for giving me my dad. I'm happy to finally have both of my parents in my life. Amen."

As Callie opened her eyes, she looked at Nigel. Found that he was staring at her.

And she thought she saw in his eyes an expression she'd seen years ago. One of affection.

But he turned quickly and smiled at Kwame. And the moment—whatever it was between them—was gone.

"Mommy, I don't feel so good," Kwame said. He was holding his stomach, and Callie wondered if he maybe had eaten something that didn't agree with him.

"Your stomach?"

Kwame nodded.

Callie felt his head for any sign of fever, and noted that he was a little warm. "You might have a slight fever, actually," she said.

"Come here, bud." Nigel approached Kwame and put his arm around his shoulder. "Why don't you let me take care of you for a moment, okay?"

This was Callie's role, taking care of her sick son. It had been for nine years. And every part of her wanted to follow him and Nigel down the hallway to his bedroom, lie him down and then get a cold compress to put on his forehead. But she also knew that Nigel wanted to be a father in every sense of the word. Not just when things were good, but when things were bad. And if Kwame was sick, this constituted as the bad.

So as much as Callie would have loved to be the one to

care for Kwame right now, she stood back and let Nigel take the lead role.

Several minutes later, Nigel appeared in the living room. Callie looked up from the sofa, asking, "How is he?"

"He's okay. Resting. I'm going to get him a glass of water."

Callie nodded, smiling softly. It was what she would do as well.

Nigel continued to the kitchen, and moments later was heading back into Kwame's bedroom with a tall glass of ice water. Callie went into the kitchen and began to scrape the dinner dishes. A minute later, Nigel was back. Callie looked toward him, and her heart filled with emotion. Nigel was such an attractive man. And not simply because of his exterior good looks—that was obvious. But because of how great he was at being a father.

That was the kind of thing a woman couldn't ignore.

He took a few steps toward her, and her breath caught in her throat. For a moment, she wondered if he was going to kiss her. Despite his talk about them moving beyond their sexual encounter.

"Is he sleeping?" Callie asked.

"Not yet, but he's going down."

Callie turned from the sink full of plates. "You really are a natural with him."

"I've always wanted to be a dad."

Nigel moved forward, holding her gaze, and Callie's heart stopped. My God, he *was* going to kiss her?

She held her breath, pressed her fingers behind her back against the countertop as he stepped forward. Waited.

But Nigel walked past her and to the fridge, which he opened and then pulled out a cold bottle of beer.

Callie's heart deflated. What was wrong with her? She didn't want him to kiss her. So what if he had just put her son down in the way that the most caring of fathers would? She was happy to know that he was a good father to their son, filling that void and Kwame's life.

But what about the void in your life? was the thought that popped into her mind.

"Want a beer?" Nigel asked.

Callie shook her head as she slowly turned back to the sink. "No. I'm fine."

She didn't need beer to cloud her judgment. Her own emotions were helping her do that just fine.

"Listen," Nigel began. "I have something to tell you. And now's as good a time as any."

Callie faced him. "It sounds serious."

"It is." Nigel paused. "I found the name of the man your mother was dating when she brought you to live with your aunt."

Callie sucked in a sharp breath. "You did?"

Nigel nodded. "He was a pretty bad guy, from all I've been able to figure out. A list of charges as long as a football field. Doesn't look like there was a day this guy wasn't involved in doing something illegal."

Callie's heart was racing. The news that Nigel had found the name of her mother's boyfriend was tampered by the reality that the guy had clearly been a thug. Why had her mother dated someone like that?

The ultimate truth at this point was that it didn't matter. What was done was done. And Callie was more interested in getting at the truth. She needed answers. If those answers revealed something dark, so be it. As long as she learned the truth about her mother.

"I've also learned that your mother was a witness against him in a court case. Well, *supposed* to be a witness against him. Before she could testify against him she ran."

So her mother had agreed to testify against this man. That

changed things, because it meant that her mother had been compelled to do the right thing.

Suddenly, Callie frowned. What if the worst had happened to her mother because of this man? Had Miriam agreed to testify and paid the price for her decision?

How many people—career criminals especially—would try to take out a witness if that meant avoiding going to jail?

"What were the charges against this person?" Callie asked. "What was my mother going to testify to?"

"This guy's name was Rodney Cook, and he was charged with fraud at the time. Like I said, he had a rap sheet a mile long. Forgery, false insurance claims, scamming senior citizens. Anything he could do to make a quick buck, he did. But he graduated from that to counterfeiting currency in a particularly elaborate scam. From what I've learned, he was involved with an organization that was distributing this counterfeit currency, and your mother was going to testify to what she knew about that."

Callie digested the information. On the grand scale of criminal actions, fraud wasn't that bad, was it? More importantly, she was thinking that someone who committed fraud wasn't likely the type to commit murder.

"Is that the worst of it? Of his crimes, I mean."

"At the time your mother was involved with him, yes. But in later years, Rodney's crimes got worse. Some drug offenses, for example. Currently, he's in jail for manslaughter."

Nigel's latest words made Callie's heart leap into her throat. There went her theory on Rodney likely not being the type to commit a violent crime. Manslaughter...if he had committed manslaughter, he could easily have killed her mother.

"Is there no sign of my mother? You say she ran, and the only reason I believe she wasn't killed—at least not initially— is because my aunt said she was in touch with her for at least a couple years after she left us in her care. Maybe she went into witness protection or something."

"Typically witness protection requires that someone testify against someone, and your mother never got to do that. Besides, it's not like this character was a major level criminal. Certainly he was a bad guy, but from my experience not the type that the government would be willing to relocate someone over. He wasn't facing huge, huge time, but I can't say for sure. I'll have to do more of an investigation."

"When did you learn all this?"

"Yesterday. I went in to the station to tie up some loose ends on a few cases. I figured I'd look into your mother's case. See what I could find."

"Where is he?" Callie asked.

"He's in federal prison in California."

Callie was silent. She was thinking. Nigel then said, "Don't think about it. Don't try doing anything silly like tracking this man down."

"I won't." But Callie wasn't certain that she wouldn't. She knew there were ways to do it, and she wasn't sure if she would be able to, but she might have to try if he held the only clues.

"I will continue looking on my end," Nigel explained. "There's got to be something somewhere about your mother and I'll find out."

"But is this normal?" Callie asked. "For someone to disappear off the grid completely?"

Nigel shook his head. "I'm not going to lie to you, Callie. It's not. And I have to acknowledge that it's not a good sign."

Emotion suddenly overwhelmed her, and Callie placed a hand on her mouth, stifling a sob.

"Hey," Nigel said. He rose and walked toward her.

"I'm sorry," Callie said. "It's just…"

"You don't have to apologize," Nigel said, and Callie met

his gaze. "I know how hard it is, the not knowing. So to hear this news…I get it."

Callie's chest shuddered as she drew in an unstable breath. "Is that what it was like for you, when I left?"

Nigel nodded. "Yeah. There were days I wondered if you were dead or alive."

Callie hadn't thought that he would be consumed with worry, and she hadn't meant to make him feel that way. Had her mother also not realized how her daughters would feel, always wondering what had happened to her?

"I guess I always thought that no matter what happened between us, you wouldn't totally cut yourself off from me."

There were no words. Callie had left because she had needed a clean break for her sanity. It had been the only way she could leave Nigel, have his child and emotionally survive.

"I know you didn't have to look into my mother's case, so thank you," she said. And then, as if of its own will, her hand landed on his chest. "It's nice to know that after everything, you still care."

"I do," Nigel uttered. Then, "Damn it."

"What?" Callie asked. Though she knew. Because an electric charge of desire had just shot through her body, and she was certain Nigel had felt it, too.

What was it about them that a simple touch could cause both of their bodies to be simultaneously turned on?

"If we're going to stick to the being-friends bit, it's best you don't touch me…like that."

Callie's fingers were moving up and down his chest, over the area of his scar. His heart.

"What if I don't want to stop touching you?" And knew she must be mad. Because words were coming from her mouth that she didn't plan.

"What are you saying?" Nigel asked, his voice low.

"I…" What *was* she saying? "I guess I didn't expect it to be this hard."

"What?" When Callie didn't speak, he went on. "Us living together?"

Not meeting his eyes, she nodded.

"Tell me about it. I feel like I'm walking around in a constant state of arousal."

Callie's eyes flew to his. "Really?"

"I guess time hasn't changed one thing," Nigel said, placing his hand on hers. "We were always good together."

"That we were," she agreed.

"And I'm not seeing anyone. Neither are you. Maybe there's no reason to fight what always came so naturally for us."

Callie found herself nodding. And before she knew it, Nigel placed his mouth on hers.

And just like the last time, her body erupted with heat. What was it about kissing Nigel that thrilled her like no one else's kisses ever had?

He framed her face and kissed her with gentle persistence, the kind of kiss Callie knew she would never get enough of.

As the kiss deepened, he moved his hands from her face, along the length of her neck and then down her arms. Finally, Callie slipped her arms around his neck, noting that her right shoulder only hurt mildly as she did so.

"Mom?"

At the sound of Kwame's voice, Callie jerked apart from Nigel and whipped her head around. Seconds later, Kwame rounded the corner into the kitchen.

What a close call! Callie thought, then hurried over to her son. "What is it, Kwame?"

"Maybe you can make me some chicken noodle soup?"

"Of course." Callie met Nigel's gaze, and his expression seemed to say the same thing she felt. *Close call.* "You have chicken noodle soup, Nigel?"

"Yeah, sure."

"Do you mind preparing it for Kwame? Because what you just told me…I should go see my sisters, fill them in. The sooner the better." Callie was aware that she was rambling, and that it was for Kwame's benefit. She didn't want him to suspect that she and Nigel had been doing anything in the kitchen other than talking.

"Right," Nigel said. "Sure."

She wasn't directly meeting his gaze. "Then I'll just go. Now."

"You do that," Nigel told her.

Callie turned to Kwame. "Your father's going to make you the soup. I need to see your aunts for a bit. Okay?"

Kwame nodded. "Okay."

Then, with one last sheepish glance at Nigel, Callie waltzed out of the kitchen, then exited the house.

Chapter 15

A short while later, Callie was telling her sisters what she had learned from Nigel.

"You're sure?" Deanna asked.

"Yes," Callie said to her sisters, who were sitting at the small kitchen table. "Nigel found our mother's former boyfriend—the one she was running from."

"Oh my Lord," Natalie said. "I've been praying for this. Praying we would find something soon."

"It's only a small step," Callie said, keeping her tone measured. "All he told me is that the man's name is Rodney Cook, and he's currently incarcerated for manslaughter."

"Then we have to go talk to him," Natalie said. "Make him tell us what happened to our mother."

Callie stared at her sister, at the obvious hope in her eyes. Even as young children, she had always been the one to be extra hopeful. Despite the clear evidence that their mother had abandoned them, Natalie had always felt she would return one day.

Deanna, however, looked more cautiously hopeful. "Did Nigel try to talk to this guy?"

"He's in prison in California," Callie explained. "A far trek."

"But a short flight away," Natalie countered.

"Did you hear what I said?" Callie asked, wondering how her sister could have missed the big picture. "The guy's in jail for *manslaughter*. Doesn't that concern you?"

As Callie stared from Natalie to Deanna, her words seemed to register. Natalie gasped.

"You don't think…you don't think he killed her?" Natalie asked. "That's not what you're saying, is it?"

"I think we need to be prepared for the worst," Callie said. "After all, even Auntie Jean said that our mother was in touch with her for a few years, then the contact just stopped."

Deanna pushed back her chair and rose, then began to pace the kitchen. She crossed her arms over her chest as she did, her expression grim.

"I guess what I'm saying is…" Callie began, "if we're going to move forward, we have to be prepared for the worst." She paused, then looked directly at Natalie. "Are you okay with that?"

A few moments passed before Natalie slowly nodded. "If she's gone, we still need to know."

Callie nodded. Now that there was a lead, and the real likelihood that they might discover what had happened to their mother, Callie wasn't sure what to feel. Because suddenly, perhaps not knowing might be the best thing.

"What's happening with you and Nigel?" Deanna asked.

At the question, Callie looked at her. "Excuse me?"

"You live in his home now so you've been spending a lot

of time together," Deanna went on. "And now he's helping to find our mother?"

Callie drew in a deep breath. She'd had the same thought as Deanna, that Nigel going to the length of looking into her mother's case signified he cared for her.

"He's being a friend," Callie said, and didn't meet her sister's eyes as she thought of the kiss. "And I appreciate his help."

"Could you have given a less political answer?" Deanna asked.

"Tell me about it," Natalie agreed. "I mean, look at your body language. Deanna mentioned Nigel and your whole body lit up." She paused. "Are you two an item again?"

"An item?" Callie said, her tone dismissive. "Good grief, no." But despite her words, she was feeling a swell of excitement in her chest. If Kwame hadn't interrupted them in the kitchen, she would have went to bed with him again. In fact, she felt distinctly sexually unsatisfied.

God help her, she was lusting after him.

"Oh my God, Natalie's right." Deanna stared at her, her expression one of surprise. "You *are* beaming."

"I'm not beam—" But Callie's words died on her lips when she realized that she was trying to suppress a smile.

As her sisters continued to stare at her, clearly expecting some kind of explanation, she said, "It's just the way he's taken so well to Kwame."

"Which means what?" Deanna asked.

"Why the twenty questions?" Callie countered.

Natalie smirked. "The look on your face is making it obvious, anyway. You and Nigel have reconnected, haven't you?"

"We had to reconnect," Callie said simply. "We're parents."

"Another political answer," Deanna chimed.

"Exactly," Deanna beamed. "Because you know that's not what I mean. I'm talking about *reconnecting* reconnecting."

Callie opened her mouth to speak, but said nothing. And then was flooded with the memory of Nigel's mouth on hers. How utterly magnificent the erotic charge to her body had been because of his touch....

"She's smitten," Deanna said. "Look at her."

"I'm not smitten," Callie said.

"All I can say," Deanna began, giving her a lopsided look, "is that I hope you're not seeing anyone else, and that Nigel isn't seeing anyone else. Because anyone else doesn't stand a chance."

"You're jumping from *A* to *Z*," Callie said.

"And poor Nigel, you can't leave him brokenhearted again," Natalie added.

Callie waved off the suggestion. "Nigel isn't going to be heartbroken over anything I do." She wanted to throttle Natalie when she shot her a look of disbelief. "It's true. How can you expect that there would be anything between us after all this time?"

"You didn't see Nigel when you left," Natalie said. "He was devastated. Came by and called every day. Wanted to know if we'd heard from you. I've never seen a man more heartbroken. Seriously, he loved you, Callie. The kind of love I've never seen a man express before."

The words hit Callie with the impact of a brick falling on her head. She hadn't thought about what Nigel had gone through when she had left, because it had been too hard to even think of him, and to hear of his pain hurt her in a way she didn't expect.

"Natalie's right," Deanna went on. "A love like that...it doesn't die."

Callie's heart thundered in her chest. She remembered Nigel's kiss, how tender yet passionate, and how it felt as if no time had passed when she was in his arms.

She had told herself for years that she was over him, but

she had to acknowledge that seeing him again had sparked something within her....

They'd made love, and it had been incredible, but Callie knew better than to expect that it meant something more than two people who once loved each other coming together one more time. Perhaps it had been about closure more than anything else. Because how could Nigel forgive her betrayal?

"A lot of time has passed," Callie argued, "and I'm not foolish enough to believe that Nigel's simply going to forgive me for having taken away his son without ever telling him he existed. Not exactly a great foundation for reconnecting, as you say."

"You never know what can happen," Natalie said. "One thing I'm certain about is that you and Nigel were always meant to be."

"If we were meant to be, then wouldn't we be together?" Callie retorted.

Sometimes her sister's overly romantic ideals annoyed her. Even in the face of having loved and lost someone to infidelity, Natalie still seemed to be the hopeless romantic she had always been before.

"Your problem then and now was that you couldn't see what you had. You never trusted anything. And I understand why. Heck, I understand better than anyone, except for Deanna. We were all in the same boat. All abandoned. I know that I did certain things simply because of what we went through. Because of my inability to trust love."

Callie looked doubtful. "Did you just say inability to trust love? You—the dreamer out of all of us?"

"And what happened to me? I ended up marrying someone who didn't love me, didn't I? A man who wanted a trophy wife to go along with his trophy life. Oh, I know love when I see it in other people. At least I think I do. But I'm the last person to know it when it comes into my own life."

"What I want to know," Deanna asked, "is do you still feel something for Nigel?"

"I didn't come back here to rekindle anything with Nigel," Callie said, speaking honestly. "I came back here for our aunt and uncle. And to do the right thing. It would be stupid of me to think that after all this time we could ever rekindle anything."

"But that doesn't answer the question of whether or not you want to," Deanna said.

Callie scowled as she stared at her sisters. "What has gotten into both of you today? Why all the questions about Nigel?"

"Because as much as Deanna and I haven't always seen eye to eye," Natalie began, "this is one thing we always agreed on. We used to talk about how much Nigel loved you. How you were so young, yet so lucky to find someone like him. I can't believe that a love that strong would die forever."

"Or die at all," Deanna chimed.

Hearing her sisters' words made Callie's stomach tighten. She couldn't help thinking about just how hard it had been when she had walked away from Nigel. She had loved him with all of her heart and soul. But then she had come to believe that their differences would keep them apart. Rather, *force* them apart one day. So she had done what she had considered the best thing.

She ran.

She ran, and she didn't look back. It was the only way to survive. A clean break. Because looking back would have been too painful each day. The wondering *what if.*

Callie knew just how hard it was to wonder what if. She had watched her sisters' hopefulness over the fact that their mother would return one day eventually fade. In fact, Callie had acted as the mother in many ways, telling them that yes, their mother loved them and that she would be back. But day by day, it became harder for her to believe her own words.

Then it became harder for Deanna to believe. Ultimately, only Natalie had clung to hope. But in the end, even the dreamer's hope had waned.

"I think the most important thing right now is our mother." Callie looked at her sisters in turn. "I didn't come back for Nigel, but I'm certainly glad that he's forming a wonderful relationship with his son. I came back for our aunt. And I came back for the both of you, too." Callie reached for her sisters' hands. "And now, it seems we're on track to finding out what may have happened to our mother. That's what I want to concentrate on."

The next day, Kwame was feeling better—so much so that he was giggling his head off in the living room while Callie sorted the dinner plates into the dishwasher in the kitchen.

She had left Kwame and Nigel playing Twister, but the laughter got the better of her curiosity, and Callie exited the kitchen. As she rounded the corner into the living room, she asked, "What is going on?"

"Get Mom!" Kwame exclaimed, his breathing ragged.

Nigel advanced, and Callie's eyes widened. She didn't know what Nigel was doing until his hands came down on her torso and he began to tickle her.

"No!" Callie screamed. Giggling, she tried her best to wriggle free. "No, please! No!"

Nigel didn't let up, and Callie fell forward, dropping to the floor in an attempt to escape his hands. "You're killing me!" she cried, jerking her body in a futile attempt to avoid being tickled. "Stop!"

Kwame jumped into the fray, and only after Callie was out of control laughing her head off, did Nigel and Kwame let up.

Callie looked at Nigel as the laughter subsided. He was still on top of her, his strong thighs spread over her hips. She suddenly realized just how suggestive their positioning was, and her breath—already coming in spurts—snagged in her chest.

He seemed to realize the same thing too, and something passed in his eyes as he stared at her. Callie felt undeniable heat spreading through her veins.

Good grief, how was it her attraction to him never ceased? But even more perplexing, she was certain that the feeling was mutual.

A love like that...it doesn't die.

"That was awesome, Dad!" Kwame raised his hand to Nigel for a high-five.

Nigel smacked his hand against his son's, and moved off of Callie. Just like that, the spell between them was broken.

Kwame then turned his attention to Callie, offering her a hand to help her to her feet. "See, Mom, it's fun to play once in a while." As Callie stood, Kwame said to Nigel, "My mom doesn't take enough time to play and laugh and have fun."

"Is that so?" Nigel asked, looking at her once more.

Callie could only imagine what he was thinking of her. That she was the same uptight person she had been ten years ago. No, she didn't have a lot of time to goof around like this. With her work and extra courses she took to better her knowledge of her field and being a single mother, she was busy. But she wasn't boring. She took time to spend with her son and create happy memories where she could. To hear Kwame say what he did actually surprised her.

"Oh!" Callie said as she jumped to her feet, her sense of smell instantly assaulted. "The cookies."

And with that, she charged toward the kitchen. She had put the cookies in the oven, and then began to fill the dishwasher.

Now, Callie threw open the oven and saw what she feared.

The chocolate chip cookies were a dark, dark brown, clearly burned.

How had all of them forgotten the cookies? A game of Twister and they had lost their minds.

They'd been having fun. The kind of fun families have together.

Yet they weren't a family. The thought made Callie's throat constrict, and she swallowed at the painful lump. She kept telling herself that she wasn't going to think about the past. She wasn't going to let herself regret what she couldn't change. But it was becoming harder and harder. Because sometimes, looking at Nigel with his son and seeing how completely intuitive and fantastic he was at being a father, she couldn't help but wonder what it would have been like to be with him all these years.

Kwame would have definitely benefited from having his father around, she knew that much.

"Darn it," Callie muttered as she dumped the hot cookie tray in the sink.

"It's okay, Mom," Kwame said, slipping his arms around her waist.

Callie looked at her son, noting not for the first time that he seemed far happier. In the past, he might fuss over burnt cookies, but now he was taking the mishap in stride.

"Do you still have more cookie dough?" Nigel asked.

Callie shook her head. "That was all of it."

"I can head out to the store, pick up more."

That was something a husband would offer to do…. "No need," Callie said. "There's always tomorrow."

Kwame left Callie's side and went to Nigel's. "I love you, Dad," he said, out of the blue. "And I love being here with you, and with Mom."

Callie wanted to caution Kwame to not get his hopes too high, but what could she say? That he shouldn't feel what he was feeling? Even she was enjoying spending this time as a family.

"I love having you here too, bud," Nigel said.

Kwame beamed. "Can we play the Xbox now?"

"Sure we can."

"Awesome!" Kwame bounded out of the kitchen.

Callie blew out a huff of air. "He's full of energy, I tell you. If I could bottle it, I'd make billions."

"I think it's great."

A beat passed. Then Callie said, "If I didn't say so before, I want you to know that I appreciate you taking time off of work for Kwame. He's having a wonderful time with you. And he's thriving in a way he hasn't before. He seems far more relaxed, confident and happy."

"You don't have to thank me. Spending time with him is important to me, too."

"I know, but still."

"He's a great kid," Nigel said, a smile touching his lips. "You've obviously done a great job raising him, which is where his confidence and happiness come from." He held her gaze before saying, "I'm glad he's mine, Callie. And I'm not just saying that. I'm proud to call him my son."

Emotion washed over Callie, both sweet and bitter. Because the last thing Nigel needed to do was give her a compliment on her parenting, considering she had left him out of his son's life.

And as she stared at him, she thought again of what her sisters had said. That a love like what she'd shared with Nigel didn't simply die.

"Thank you," Callie said softly.

And the bitter feeling ebbed away, replaced by an emotion that felt a lot like love.

Chapter 16

"Look at them," Callie said, gesturing to Kwame and his new friend Nathan as they frolicked in the pool. She and Nigel were sitting at the patio table, keeping watch. "Kwame's having the time of his life."

"Marry me."

Callie jerked her gaze from her son and gaped at Nigel. "W-what?"

"Marry me, Callie."

Callie simply stared at Nigel, not believing his words. This was coming out of left field. "You want to *marry* me?"

"You said yourself that Kwame is thriving being here with me. And you heard what he said last night—he said he's happy to have both of his parents in his life. It hit me last night that you could be heading back to Florida at any time, and I have to tell you, I'm not thrilled about the idea that you'll leave and I'll get to see Kwame only some of the time. I've already missed out on nine years."

Callie had always hoped that when a man proposed to her, it would be because he was crazy in love with her. But what Nigel was suggesting was a union so that they could give Kwame a traditional family.

Nigel added, "You say you came back to do the right thing. And now that I've gotten used to the fact that I'm a father, I can tell that Kwame needs me. You leave and head back to Florida, and who knows how that will affect him? Do you have any idea how much more often young kids out on the street who don't have fathers get into trouble?"

"I'm very aware of that," Callie said.

"Kwame's a great kid," Nigel continued. "But even great boys get into trouble without positive male role models. He needs me in his life. And I need him."

What Nigel *wasn't* saying was making all the difference. He wasn't telling Callie that he needed *her*.

"I understand that you want to be a permanent part of Kwame's life, and I won't keep you from him. But—"

"Don't deny me. Don't deny me this, the right to be a father in my son's life."

Callie waited. Waited for any indication that his marriage proposal was about her. But he said nothing else.

And Callie's heart deflated. Because somewhere along the way, her feelings for Nigel had resurfaced. Oh, it was glaringly clear that they'd never died. She had run to escape them, but being near him again, living with him, she was unable to forget the feelings she'd repressed.

There was a time when Callie would have relished the idea of marrying Nigel. But to know that he was proposing simply because of a sense of duty…could she really marry him?

Callie knew she'd screwed things up, but at the end of the day, when she got married, she wanted it to be because she loved someone and he loved her back.

"I think there's a way we can work something out," Callie

said. "I never saw myself coming back to Cleveland, but maybe that's what I have to do. I can apply for job here, get a place—"

"Marriage," Nigel said, leaving no room for the discussion of anything less.

Callie's rational brain told her that she owed it to him to seriously consider marriage, given that she'd kept him out of Kwame's life. But she said, "That's a big step."

"Maybe things in my life happened for a reason," Nigel said, glancing away briefly. "Two years ago, I was supposed to get married. But Angie, my fiancée, got cold feet. She suddenly didn't want to be tied down. And she was also terrified about the fact that she was marrying a police officer. She was scared that being the wife of a cop meant having to wait by the phone every time I was at work. She told me more than once that she couldn't deal with getting that dreaded call. So it didn't work out."

"You were engaged?" Callie asked, her heart beating a little faster. She didn't know why she was surprised by that fact. Nigel was a good-looking man, and a great catch. Certainly he could've been married by now and the father of other children.

Indeed, that had been a part of Callie's fear over the years when she had thought of him, wondered if she should let him know that he was a father. In part, she had dismissed the thought because she didn't want to disrupt the life he might have had with another woman.

"We dated for a year and a half before we got engaged."

"And she called it off because she was afraid?"

"Seems like a pattern in my life," Nigel said, giving her a pointed look.

"I just mean…maybe she'll be back."

"She won't be back. She got engaged to someone else six months after we broke up."

"Oh." Why did that make Callie feel better?

Though she couldn't help wondering how deeply Nigel had loved this woman. As much as he had loved her?

"Anyway, I didn't see at the time that it was a blessing for us to go our separate ways, but now that you're back, and I'm a father...I think getting married is the right thing to do."

Right thing to do.... It couldn't be clearer that his proposal had nothing to do with love.

And here she had foolishly begun to hope, in part because of the definite chemistry she had felt with Nigel, and in part because her sisters had let her know how much Nigel had been crushed by her leaving. Then, all Deanna's and Natalie's talk about a love like what she'd had with Nigel never dying....

Obviously, it *had* died. And Callie knew that she was entirely to blame.

"Callie?" Nigel prompted.

"I don't know what to say," Callie said. "All I can tell you is that I'll think about it."

Callie's rejection of his proposal was all that Nigel could think about later that day. She and Kwame went to visit extended family for a cookout, and Nigel had opted to stay home. He hadn't been in the mood to make nice with anyone, not when his conversation with Callie had him in a funk.

Nigel could tell that Callie had wanted more of him, more of a proposal, and for that reason, he knew he shouldn't be unhappy that she hadn't been jumping up and down with excitement. Nigel had wanted nothing more than a real marriage with Callie—ten years ago. But a lot had changed in ten years.

The one thing that *hadn't* changed was the fact that he still had feelings for her. That was obvious every time he looked at her, touched her, and God help him, whenever he kissed her. But Nigel couldn't allow himself to be the same kind of fool he'd been ten years earlier.

It wasn't that he wanted a marriage to Callie to be in name only forever. He did want to grow to love her again, to trust her again, and be a family in the true sense of the word. But at this point, he couldn't simply allow her to have his whole heart, not after what she'd done with it the first time around.

The fact that he was even willing to marry her should tell her that on some level he was trying to work toward forgiving her.

He had heard Callie and Kwame as they got home late in the evening, but Nigel had stayed in his room, not wanting to face her. Now, however, just after one in the morning, Nigel found himself getting out of his bed and heading to Kwame's room to check on him.

His son was sleeping peacefully, the sound of his heavy breathing filling the room. How quickly Nigel had gotten used to living with Kwame and having him be a part of his life. After only a few short weeks, it was clear that he did not want to have to go back to the status quo. He wanted Kwame in his life, and Kwame had totally accepted that.

Kids were amazing that way. They could forgive easily, accept easily. And Kwame had accepted him as his father without any hesitation.

Nigel paused outside Callie's door. The one downside to their living together was that he often thought about entering her room in the middle of the night and making love to her. And tonight, perhaps because of her rejection, he craved her body against his.

But Nigel continued back to his own room. He wasn't stupid. The more he engaged in physical intimacy with Callie, the more he lost his heart to her. And he wouldn't give his heart to her again...not yet. Because despite what his heart and body might feel for her, he had no idea if she had resolved her deep-seated issues from years ago that had caused her to run in the first place.

Nigel had just crawled back under his covers when he heard a soft knock at his door. Callie? It had to be her, not Kwame.

At one in the morning, what could she want? Had she heard him outside her door?

Nigel got up from the bed, crossed the room to the door and opened it. Callie stood there, looking up at him with a vulnerable expression. She was wearing an oversized T-shirt and nothing else. Nigel's gaze couldn't help wandering to her bare legs.

A part of him wanted to take her in his arms and never let her go. He couldn't deny that ever since she had come back into his life, some of what he felt for her in the past had come back full force.

"Yes?" he said.

Callie's eyes wandered over his body, over his bare chest and to his thighs. Dressed for bed, he was wearing only boxers.

Her gaze left him feeling hot and bothered.

"I was thinking about what you said," Callie said. "That we should get married."

She had thought all evening about his suggestion. That was how she saw it, because she didn't consider it a proposal. She was willing to atone for her sins in the most sincere way, and if that meant that she had to uproot her life to make it up to Nigel, she would.

"I agree with you," Callie went on. "It's in Kwame's best interest to be able to spend quality time with you, to have you in his life on more than a part-time basis."

"Good."

Callie's eyes swept over Nigel again. Damn, he was looking especially tempting. Standing there wearing only his boxers, all she could think about was when they'd made love…and that she wanted to do it again.

"I—I came here to talk a bit more about your suggestion."

"At one-twenty in the morning?"

She nodded, though that wasn't entirely true. She had heard him in the hallway, and ever since yesterday when he'd straddled her as he'd tickled her, Callie had been aroused, ready to make love to him. But his marriage proposal had thrown her for a loop, and she had come to his room to tell Nigel that if he didn't want to marry her for the right reasons, she couldn't go through with it.

Instead, all she could think about right now was getting naked.

"Are you saying you've made your decision?" Nigel asked her.

So dispassionate, Callie thought. Did he feel nothing for her? Was there nothing inside him that remembered the fire they generated when they got together? And not just the physical fire. That was a given. But the fierce emotional connection they'd shared.

Suddenly, she had to know. She had to know if what they had shared before still existed for him.

She had fallen into bed with him, but that had been a moment of need. She'd been vulnerable when she had run off in the rain, and Nigel had reacted instinctively. The same way he had in the past. Protecting her.

Tonight, she wanted to see if there was still something between them beyond the physical. She had definitely felt a growing emotional connection ever since the first time they'd made love after all those years. Not only had Nigel made love to her with the kind of passion that made her believe he had to care, he had gone out of his way to look into her mother's disappearance. Surely he still cared for her.

Callie wanted to believe that Nigel cared, but the truth was that men were different than women. They could have sex without any emotion.

"Callie?" Nigel said.

"Tell me you feel nothing for me," she found herself saying.

Nigel's eyes widened in surprise. She took a step toward him, closing the distance between them. She placed her hands on his naked chest, and felt that familiar physical charge. His strong pecs, those washboard abs—he was a magnificent specimen. He always had been.

"What are you doing?"

"You say you want to marry me. In name only? Or more than that?"

She didn't allow him to answer. Instead, she slid her arms and hands up his chest and around his neck. She had taken her sling off two days ago, ready to be done with it, and it felt good to press her body against Nigel's without restrictions.

She tipped herself onto her toes and leaned into him. Her need to taste this man once more was overpowering. She was aware that Nigel's lips parted, and she took the opportunity to put her mouth on his.

She sighed with pleasure as he enveloped her completely. This was real. For her, these feelings had never died. Her feelings for Nigel were as intense as before. Her body and his body together equaled magic.

His lips began to respond, mating with hers in a dance as old as time. And when his hands gently framed her face— oh, how his touch thrilled her—she purred into his mouth.

He groaned and deepened the kiss, delving his tongue into her mouth with broad strokes. It swept over hers, eliciting even more delicious sensations within her. The kiss picked up speed, becoming more urgent with each passing second. She wanted this more than she had wanted anything.

She dragged her fingernails down his back, knowing that she was being perhaps a little too rough but not able to stop herself. She would physically embed herself with him, meld their bodies together for all time if she could. Nigel had always made her feel complete in a way that she had never felt since.

"Tell me you feel something," she rasped as she tore her lips from his. "Tell me I'm not imagining there's still a connection between us."

"No. You're not imagining it."

And as Nigel pulled her into his arms, emotion overwhelmed her. Tears filled her eyes as she thought of the fact that this was exactly where she wanted to be. With this man for all time.

How stupid she had been to let her fear keep them apart.

Kissing her with fiery need, Nigel lifted her into his arms and brought her to the bed. As he lay her down, his lips moved from her mouth to the underside of her jaw. His full, sensuous lips pleased her skin. He used his teeth and his tongue, and Callie thought she would die from the pleasure.

She was wearing only a T-shirt, and Nigel slipped his hands beneath it and ran his warm palms along her thighs, up to her hips, and then her torso. And when he reached her breasts, she sighed again.

"Time and distance may have come between us," Callie said in a throaty voice, "but this—the way we connect—is still the same."

"We were always great together," Nigel agreed.

Callie smiled as she moaned. She eased herself up, placing her hands on his chest. "Take off my clothes."

Without waiting for more encouragement, Nigel reached for her hands and urged her to her feet. Standing in front of her, he took either side of her T-shirt in his palms and pulled it over her head.

"Yes," Callie moaned when her breasts were exposed.

Nigel made a sound of pleasure. His hands went to her

hips, and he worked her lacy panties down her thighs and tossed them onto the floor, as well.

Naked, his eyes swept over her, and Callie felt herself get even hotter than before. She wondered if this was how people felt before they spontaneously combusted. Because the molten heat flowing through her body now was scorching.

"You're even more beautiful now than before," Nigel told her.

His words were music to her ears.

Nigel reached for her breasts, played with her nipples until she was moaning. But that wasn't enough for her. She needed him to make to love to her.

So despite her pleasure and the selfish desire to let Nigel stroke and caress her all night long, she pulled at his boxers. When they were around his thighs, she reached for his erection. She stroked him urgently, not caring about the art of the tease. Right now was about fire and passion and spending the night proving they still felt something for each other.

He stepped backward so that he could work his boxers the rest of the way down his legs. Then he kicked them off. Within moments, he was standing before her naked, and Callie felt the biggest rush. How was it that after all this time, after leaving him because she'd been too afraid to stay and fight for their relationship, that she still felt as wildly passionate about this man as she had years earlier?

He moved toward her, and she did the same, the two of them coming together in a fury of passion. His arms wrapped around her body, sliding up and down her back. She slipped her arms around his waist, reveling in the feel of his muscles. As her hands moved to his back and ventured down to his tight buttocks, Nigel's hands roamed over her behind, as well. But his hands quickly went from her behind around to the front of her torso and up her rib cage, and then over the mounds of her breasts, eliciting the deepest moan of pleasure from her.

His touch electrified her, turned her on more than anything.

With a growl, Nigel tore his lips from hers and moved his mouth down to her breasts. While his fingers tweaked her nipples, his mouth kissed the mounds of flesh.

She wanted more. She wanted to feel his mouth on her peaks of pleasure, enjoy the sensations that she knew his tongue would elicit. He was teasing her, drawing out her pleasure.

"I—I can't take it. Stop teasing me."

"I know, baby. You never could take too much of my torturing you like this."

"Never. Please…"

"As you wish." Obeying her demand, Nigel brought his mouth down on one nipple and drew it into the moist recesses of his mouth completely. He suckled it hard, the sensation pure bliss.

Callie's hands dug into his back so hard she was sure she'd broken the skin. But she didn't care. She wanted to brand him with the experience they were sharing. Give him something to remember.

"I've missed this, Nigel. I didn't know how much."

Nigel brought his mouth to her other breast, and she made another moaning sound, almost like weeping. It was the kind of sound that said she had never experienced desire like this for anyone else.

Her sounds of pleasure urged Nigel on. He wanted to do more than please her. He wanted to make the moment last forever. He had always loved how Callie had responded to him. Those delectable little sounds she made that let him know how turned on she was.

He couldn't deny that this explosive heat between them was real. And like a moth to a flame, he couldn't stay away. He could spend hours in bed with her and never be bored. Spend hours in bed with her and still want more.

That reality scared him. Because he had given this woman his heart once, and she had destroyed it.

And yet, his passion for her had not waned. It made no sense.

All Nigel knew, as he slipped his hands between her thighs and was rewarded with a shuddering moan, was that some things couldn't be explained. Perhaps no time, no distance, no betrayal was too great to make the body forget just how good it felt in a certain person's arms.

She was gripping his shoulders now, whimpering as she used his strength to hold her up. His mouth was pleasuring her breasts and his hands were pleasuring her center, and he knew all too well she would explode any moment. She loved this. This torture, as she used to call it. And as much as he wanted to take her right now, make her his in the way that men had done since Adam and Eve, he held back. He allowed himself to simply pleasure her, feel his own sense of satisfaction as he could hear her climax building.

"Please…"

The words were a soft cry, and quickly turned into a long and rapturous moan. He held her as she succumbed to her orgasm, her body too weak to fight it off any longer. Only once he was absolutely certain that she had experienced every ounce of pleasure that she could, did he sweep her into his arms and take her to the bed. She was breathing raggedly, unable to speak, but her sounds told him everything he needed to understand. That for her as for him, no one else had ever been able to make this experience so meaningful.

Nigel lowered himself onto the bed on top of her, settled

between her thighs, and then thrust into her like a man who had waited his entire life for this.

"Oh, baby!" Callie cried.

The words were magic to his ears. He began to love her with the hard and steady strokes she had always enjoyed. Soon, they were moving together, finding their rhythm. And it felt incredible, being with her like this in a way that Nigel never would have believed possible again. Not after how she had walked out on him.

He opened his eyes and stared down at her, saw that she was looking at him. His breath caught in his chest. She was a vision of loveliness. Absolutely stunning. Her eyes were smoky, filled with desire for him…had a woman ever been more beautiful?

She reached up a hand and stroked his face, a gentle caress. The touch stirred something in his soul. Something that he'd been trying to ignore ever since she had shown up at his door.

He tried to block that thought as he continued to make love to her, and concentrated instead on the feelings flowing through his body. He didn't want to think about tomorrow nor the past. All he wanted to think about right now was *this*. And *this* was incredible.

Callie tightened her legs around his waist, and as he caught her gaze, she smiled at him. Oh yes, she remembered their lovemaking all too well. Remembered the very things that turned him on. As she kept her feet locked behind his buttocks, the pace increased, growing faster. Her moans grew deeper, and so did his. His breathing became more ragged. And as he sensed another orgasm building within her, just as he had so many other times in the past, he rode the wave with her, the both of them falling into a fiery pit of desire together.

Chapter 17

It was dark when Callie awoke, and she was hardly well rested, but still she felt like a new woman.

She knew instantly where she was. In Nigel's arms. A place she'd never expected to be again.

She knew she wasn't dreaming. Her body ached in too many places for the memory of what had happened between them to be a dream. And she had the answer to the question she had gone in search of last night, she was sure. The passion between them hadn't died. And if the passion hadn't died, didn't that mean there were still feelings between them? Surely passion couldn't be that strong without love.

Because that's what this was about for her. As wonderful as their lovemaking had been, Callie knew that she only felt the explosive desire with him because he still had her heart. He still had her heart, even after all this time.

Perhaps it was crazy, and she was terrified of the truth. But as Nigel's arms snaked around her waist and pulled her closer, she couldn't help thinking that even in sleep, he was giving her the answer she desired.

She still had his heart, as well.

A short while later, Callie could no longer sleep. The clock said it was almost six in the morning, and she didn't want Kwame to wake up and find her and Nigel in bed together.

She quietly called out to Nigel, but he didn't wake, so Callie carefully got out of his bed and returned to her own bedroom. Only once in her own bed could she sleep again.

When she awoke later, bright sunlight was filtering into her room. And she was still smiling. What a night she'd had with Nigel! Last night had marked a turning point with them.

Glancing at the clock, she saw that it was after nine. Surely Kwame was up by now.

So Callie got up, slipped into a robe, and then exited her room. She made her way down the hallway, her mind registering the sound of voices as she got closer to the opening that led to the living room. It took her a nanosecond to realize that Nigel and Kwame were talking. She slowed, suddenly aware that if they were having a father-son talk, she didn't want to interrupt.

"…marry my mom?" Callie heard her son ask.

Callie quietly slipped a little farther backward when she heard the question Kwame had asked. She held her breath as she waited for Nigel to answer.

"Remember I told you before that my relationship with your mother is complicated?"

"Yeah."

"I want to be there for you," Nigel said. "I want us to be a strong family unit. I am determined to be the dad you need in your life. So yes, I want to marry your mom."

Callie's heart deflated a little. After last night, she had expected Nigel to proudly claim that he wanted to marry her because he loved her.

"Do you love her?" Kwame asked.

Now Callie's heart began to pound. He was going to say yes. Certainly he would…

There was a long pause. "I will tell you that your mother and I both love you very much, and right now, you're the most important person in this situation. No matter what happens between your mother and me, I don't want you to worry because I'll always be there for you. Understand?"

Callie's heart sank. *Do you love my mom?* It needed a simple yes or no answer. And Nigel had not been able to say yes.

Callie scurried back down the hallway to the bedroom, where she returned to her bed with a wretched feeling in the pit of her stomach. She'd spent the night making love with Nigel and had been convinced that he had felt about her the same way that she felt about him.

Because she loved him. She had no doubts about that. And more than anything, she wanted him in her life again.

The way he'd made love to her, she thought for sure that he was ready to forgive her and move on with her as a couple. But apparently, last night had been about a physical release for Nigel, nothing more.

Because if he loved her, surely he would put Kwame's mind at ease by telling him so.

And he hadn't. She couldn't sugarcoat that, no matter how much she wanted to.

Callie rolled onto her side, hugging her torso as she did. If at this point Nigel didn't know that he loved her, then he never would.

Tears filled Callie's eyes as the brutal reality hit her. She was distressed. Though she had never expected Nigel to forgive her when she had first told him her secret, he had finally made her believe that he would. And now, after daring to hope, she wasn't prepared for the reality of what it felt like to know that Nigel wouldn't forgive her.

God help her, knowing that he wanted to marry her only so that he could be a father to Kwame...

Callie stifled a cry. She couldn't marry him. She was the type of woman who wanted all or nothing.

She would never keep Nigel from his son. There was no need to get married simply for him to be in Kwame's life on a permanent basis. She loved her son, and she would do what was best for him. But if she was going to marry someone, it had to be because she loved that person and that person loved her back. A marriage of convenience—which was clearly what Nigel had proposed—simply would not do. And it *wouldn't* be a good thing for Kwame, who would feel confused as he witnessed their dispassionate relationship.

No, Callie couldn't play house with him. Not now that she had fallen in love with him again. Because it would hurt horribly to marry a man she still loved, knowing that he didn't love her back.

Besides, if he married her but didn't love her, how soon before he resented her? And before she resented him, as well? Because she would not feel good sharing his bed at times, knowing that ultimately he didn't love her the way she needed him to love her. It would be too painful.

Callie's chest hurt when she breathed. It was clear that he was still physically attracted to her, but he couldn't get over the hurdle of her betrayal. And at the end of the day, that was her fault. She was the one who had left Nigel. She couldn't expect him to love her as though she had never walked away from him.

She couldn't expect it, but she had hoped for that. Especially with a child in the mix.

"Idiot," Callie said to herself. How foolish she was to

believe that a couple hot nights of passion—tender passion that reminded her of all the good things they had shared as younger lovers—meant anything. The woman who prided herself on not being a hopeless romantic had gotten caught up in romantic ideals.

And wasn't that exactly why she had walked away from him before? Because she knew that to hope for the best was setting yourself up for disaster? She had totally feared that if she had stayed with him, he would leave her one day.

And yet here she was, having set herself up for disaster by believing that she and Nigel could have a second chance at love.

Tears fell from her eyes now, even though she didn't want them to. But she couldn't pretend that she wasn't affected by this. Because she was.

If only Nigel could have told Kwame that he loved her but that they were still working their relationship out. That was what mattered. Because if you loved someone, you could get through anything.

As the thought popped into her mind, Callie thought of the irony. Ten years ago, she hadn't believed that if you loved someone you could get through anything.

Or maybe she simply hadn't been able to trust in love.

Callie had already made the calls to set up an interview with the Cleveland board of education. She was willing to relocate here because it was something she could do more easily than Nigel likely could. Even though she would miss everyone in Florida at her high school there, she knew she owed it to her son.

But now, she was rethinking that. Maybe she could go back to Florida after all. Just make sure that she allowed Nigel to spend as much time with Kwame as possible.

She was thinking about that when a knock at the door

startled her. Quickly wiping her tears, she sat up, and called, "Yes?"

"Can I come in?"

Her heart pounded at the sound of Nigel's voice. She needed to get over him the way he had gotten over her. No matter how many years she put between them, clearly her heart still held a torch for him.

"Yes," she answered, wiping even more tears. "Come in."

She was taken aback when she saw Nigel and Kwame, Kwame holding a tray on which there were pancakes, and Nigel carrying a tall glass of orange juice and a mug of what she assumed was coffee. "Kwame wanted to bring you breakfast in bed," Nigel said.

"Oh."

"You weren't getting up," Nigel went on. "So he thought this would be a nice treat for you."

Callie's heart hurt. She had to hold in her tears. She couldn't handle this. She couldn't handle this kind of idealistic family scenario. She couldn't handle him playing father and husband. It made it all the more clear just how much she was missing out on.

But she forced a smile. "That was very sweet of you," she said, trying to talk past the lump of emotion that had lodged in her throat. "Very sweet indeed."

"Don't cry, Mommy," Kwame said.

Callie's eyes flew to her son's. *Was* she crying?

The next thing she knew, Nigel was wiping at the tears that had fallen, and his gentle fingers against her skin once again reminded her of everything she loved about him. Reminded her of how incredible last night had been in his arms.

"I'm just…I'm touched that you would do this for me."

"You don't need to cry," Kwame told her. "We're a family now. Dad and I are gonna do this for you lots of times from now on. Right, Dad?"

"You bet," Nigel agreed.

That's exactly the problem, Callie thought. It was one thing to accept treatment like this from someone who loved you. But from someone who wouldn't give you their complete heart…it was painful.

But Callie said none of that. Her son was beaming at her, and Nigel was looking at her with fondness. If she hadn't overheard what he'd said to her son a short time ago, she would have mistaken the look for love.

"Thank you," Callie said. "Thank you both."

Callie ate her breakfast alone in her room, and half an hour later, Nigel returned to collect the tray of dishes.

"You don't have to do that," Callie said.

"Kwame wanted to do the whole shebang. Said it shouldn't just be Mother's Day that you get special treatment. Of course, he's outside with Nathan, so…"

"So you get the job of cleaning the dishes."

"Pretty much."

Not meeting his eyes, Callie nodded. "Hmm."

"Are you okay?" Nigel asked.

"Yeah. Sure."

"No, I don't think so. You seem…different this morning. Something's bothering you."

"Why would I be different this morning?" Callie replied, crossing her arms over her chest as she moved to stand by the window.

"I don't know. But compared to last night—"

"Last night, you made love to me as though you still cared about me," Callie interjected, whirling around. "Today, I have no clue what to think. Last night I thought maybe we had a chance. That maybe you had forgiven me. That there was truly some hope for a future between us."

Nigel's eyes narrowed. "I don't understand."

"I heard you," Callie explained. "This morning. I heard you talking with my son. He asked you if you loved me, and you couldn't say that you did. You told him you wanted to marry me to make sure he had a home, a stable family, but that was it."

"Did you hear yourself?" Nigel asked, giving her pointed look.

"Of course I did."

"*My* son. You said *my* son." He paused, let the comment wash over her. "You say I'm not totally committed to us, and how can I be? When you can't even see Kwame as *our* son."

"That—that doesn't mean anything," Callie said, but her voice caught temporarily. "For nine years, it's been just me and Kwame. Old hab—"

"You don't have to tell me that," Nigel said sourly.

"So you'll never forgive?" Disappointment filled Callie's heart as she looked at him. Why had he bothered to get her hopes up at all? And why had he made love to her as though he still felt something for her when clearly all he felt was bitterness?

"I'm trying to do the right thing," Nigel told her. "I want to be a father to my son."

Pain roiled through Callie's stomach, as piercing as if she was trying to digest a bowling ball. Any other time, a woman hearing the absentee father of her child say that he wanted to be in his child's life would most likely be cause for celebration. But now, hearing Nigel make clear his motive for marrying her, Callie only felt brokenhearted.

"You can be," she said, trying to keep the emotion out of her voice. "I already told you I'm committed to seeing that happen."

"Good. Then say you'll marry me."

Callie closed her eyes, finding it hard to breathe. Again, she thought of how this situation was the complete opposite of what it should be. The man she loved asking her to marry him, and she was feeling distress over that fact.

But if Nigel didn't love her, how could she marry him?

He doesn't love me. The very thought stung. How foolish Callie had been to quickly let herself get caught up in emotions. To quickly start to hope.

She should have known better.

And yet a small flame of hope still burned. She found herself saying, "What about me? I know you want to be there for Kwame, but what about me? Us?"

Nigel stared at her, not speaking. Callie lowered her hands from her chest, waiting for Nigel to say something. To tell her that she was wrong to think he didn't care. That he *did* feel something for her.

But he remained quiet. He stood there looking at her, not saying a word. Which said everything.

"I see," Callie said, her voice hoarse. She knew she was on the verge of losing it.

She'd needed to hear him say that he loved her, that he was determined to work past their differences. Because if he didn't love her, then she couldn't bear to be with him any longer, playing a family. That would only lead to more heartbreak than she was already experiencing.

"So last night," Callie went on, because she needed to know. "What exactly was last night?"

Nigel was silent for a long moment. Then he said, "You know what last night was."

"I do?" Callie scoffed.

"You should," Nigel told her.

"Really? Okay, I'll tell you what I thought. I thought…" She paused, suddenly unable to go on. It hurt to voice the thought she'd had, knowing how wrong she had been.

"You thought what?"

"I thought last night…what we did was about love. But

obviously for you it was just about…I don't know, convenience?"

She looked at Nigel, imploring him to tell her that she was wrong. That of course last night he had felt love.

But he said nothing, just looked downcast with an expression that said he was conflicted.

"Well, there you go. That sums it up in a nutshell, doesn't it? I'm not an idiot, and that's why I can't marry you."

Finally, Nigel reacted with a look other than ambiguity. "What?" he asked.

"Do you love me?" Callie gave him a pointed stare. It was a challenge really. "If you tell me that you love me, then we can get married."

Groaning, Nigel ran a hand over his head. "Why are you making this difficult? We need to do what's right for Kwame."

The last light of hope was blown out. How many times had she given Nigel a chance to say that he cared? It wouldn't bother her if he told her that they had a lot to work on, as long as he could tell her that she was still the woman in his heart.

"I won't keep your son from you," Callie began softly.

"Come on, Callie. You can't expect this to be easy for me. I'm trying. The very fact that I'm willing to marry you—"

"*Willing*?" Callie asked, Nigel's comment the nail in the proverbial coffin. "I don't want you to be *willing* to marry me."

"No, you just want me to trust you implicitly. To forget everything you did and how that devastated me. Well, I *want* to trust you. I want our relationship to be what it was. That's why I proposed marriage. Because I want to try. But you can't expect me to simply say that, yeah, I feel one hundred percent the way I felt ten years ago, with no doubts at all. What happens when something else goes wrong that you don't like? You gonna run again? Then where will I be?"

Callie said nothing. Nigel's words struck a chord. She knew she had run before. But despite their differences over what happened to her friend back then, the bigger issue had been fear. Fear that loving Nigel totally and completely would lead to heartbreak because he would one day leave her.

The way her mother had left her.

"I know I left you," Callie said, "and that I was wrong to do what I did. But you weren't perfect, Nigel."

"Whatever you didn't like, why didn't you talk to me about it back then?"

"After you accused me of sleeping with Jeremiah?" Callie shot back.

"What?"

"I was so upset about his death, and you accused me of sleeping with him."

Nigel narrowed his eyes, confused. And then realization dawned. "I didn't accuse you of sleeping with Jeremiah. Not seriously."

"Oh, really?"

"You were so angry with me for deciding to join the police force, citing what had happened to Jeremiah. It was an off-the-cuff comment. But you're not going to tell me that *that's* why you left me."

"That you would even say that hurt me, Nigel. It made me realize you didn't trust me."

"Wow." Nigel shook his head. "After all this time, *this* is your excuse for walking away from me and not telling me about our son?"

"I'm pointing out that you had your flaws, too."

"It's an excuse. But I'll tell ya, I had hoped that you'd come up with something better than that for leaving."

"That wasn't the only reason. You know that."

"What I know is that you left me with a broken heart and a ton of questions."

Callie and Nigel stared each other down for several seconds. Then Nigel broke the silence. "You think I don't know you, but I do. And I see in your face the same fear I saw before. The same fear that caused you to run." He paused. "I want to do the right thing. I want things to work out because right now, Kwame has to come first. But the truth is, I don't know that we'll ever recapture what we had before you left ten years ago."

More silence ensued, in which Callie had no idea what to say. Then her phone rang, the distraction startling her. But when she went to pick it up from the night table and saw Tamara's number, she was glad. She needed someone else to talk to, someone else's problem to focus on.

She picked up the phone and turned to Nigel. "I have to take this call."

"Of course you do."

And then he turned and left the room.

As if he had the only right to be upset! Callie alone wasn't going to take the blame for their relationship's failure. Not this time. She had made love to him last night, and it had been about love. Not about convenience. Not about hoping. But about feeling. About recapturing what they had once had and being willing to move forward as a family unit out of love.

The time to tell her that he didn't think they would ever recapture what they'd had ten years ago was *before* he had slept with her, not the morning after.

She had given him herself completely, hoping that he would see into her heart and the fact that she still loved him.

In fact, she had never stopped loving him. That was completely clear to her now.

"Hello? Are you there?"

Hearing Tamara's voice sounding through the phone line, Callie realized that she had pressed the talk button but had not put the phone to her ear. Nigel had still consumed her thoughts.

"Hey," Callie said, trying to sound bright. "What's going on?"

Tamara began to cry, and Callie was instantly alarmed. "Hey," she repeated. "What is it? What happened?"

"It's Patrick," Tamara explained. "He—he went to my parents' house in Georgia. He was like a madman. He broke windows. He was crazy, demanding to see me, demanding that they tell him where I was."

"And did they?" Callie asked, holding her breath.

"No. No, of course not."

"Good," Callie said.

"No, it's not good," Tamara said. "I can't have Patrick terrorizing my family. I can't have him hurting the people I love. All this will go away if I go back to him."

"No," Callie told her. "No, it won't. Don't think that. Patrick threatened me and now your parents. Don't you see that he'll do anything to get you to cave to his will? Don't you see that he's as dangerous as ever? You need to stick to the plan. The police will track him down, and when they do, you make sure you go ahead and testify against him. It's the only way."

"What if I testify against him and nothing happens? Then what? He doesn't go to jail, and he's angrier than ever with me. It doesn't matter how long they lock him up. A year, ten. Once he's free, he'll come find me, and then what will he do?" Tamara paused. "No, I have to do something different, because what I've been doing isn't working. All he wants is a chance—"

"No!" Callie interjected. "Do not change from the plan. Jail is where he needs to be. Trust me, he is dangerous."

"He loves me," Tamara said. "He just wants his family back. Fear has him acting like this. He's scared."

"Tamara—"

"It's too late," Tamara said. "I've already told him I'm ready to work things out."

No, no, no. Her friend couldn't do this. She was scared, understandably so. But caving to a man like Patrick would get her nowhere but a pine box. He would know that he could totally and completely control her, and if she didn't do exactly as he pleased, he would abuse her into submission. Callie was certain of that.

"Where are you?" Callie asked. "Tell me where you are, and I'll come to you. We'll do this together, okay?" She paused. "Have you told Patrick where you are?"

"No. Not yet."

"Good. Don't tell him. Promise me that. Let me come to see you. We'll deal with this together, and you won't have to be afraid. Okay?"

Tamara didn't respond, just made a sniffling sound on the other end of the line. Callie repeated, "Okay?"

"Okay," Tamara agreed softly. "I won't tell him anything. I will wait for you to get here and then we'll figure things out."

Callie expelled a breath of relief. She knew her friend, and could tell from her voice that she was wavering. Which meant it was more important than ever for Callie to get to her.

Tamara was scared. Understandably, she didn't want to see anything bad happen to those she cared about. But going back to a man like Patrick—one who was threatening her for another chance—was a recipe for disaster. Tamara needed physical support right now. Callie would join her in Tallahassee to make sure that she didn't do anything crazy. Because there was no doubt in Callie's mind that Tamara could end up dead if she went back to Patrick. He was far too volatile and unpredictable.

Jealous people did crazy things. Hurtful things.

"You're still in Tallahassee right?" Callie asked. "At the same rental house I arranged for you?"

"Yeah."

"Give me the address, because I don't have it on me. It's still early. Depending on flight availability, I expect to be at your place this evening, or tomorrow at the latest."

Tamara recited the address, and Callie wrote it down. Before Callie hung up, she said "I'm here for you. You don't have to be afraid. Do not do anything until I get there. No texting Patrick, no answering his phone calls. Tell your parents to make sure they call the police the first sign of any trouble. Okay?"

"Okay," Tamara agreed.

Callie knew she needed to get to her friend right away. And given the tension between her and Nigel, she was actually happy for the distraction.

She would head to Tallahassee alone. After Patrick had run her off the road with Kwame in the car, the last thing Callie wanted to do was bring her son along. Not that she anticipated any problems, but this was grown folks business, and Kwame didn't need to be a part of it.

And she certainly didn't need to bring Kwame along when he had a father here who could care for him. One whom he had become extremely attached to. One he was enjoying spending more time with.

She would tell Nigel that a friend of hers was in crisis, that she needed to go away for a couple days, and confirm with him that he would be able to watch Kwame for that time. If not, between Nigel and her sisters who were still in town, Kwame would be well taken care of.

She made her way out of her bedroom and found Nigel in the backyard with Kwame. They were sitting at the patio table, simply talking. Nathan must have gone home. A smile touched Callie's lips as she regarded them. Father and son, having a simple conversation. It was the kind of thing that meant the world to her. It had changed her son's life, getting to know his father like this.

The smile soon morphed into something else, as emotion caught in her chest. She loved this man. She knew she did. She wanted nothing more than for him to say he loved her back. Then she would marry him.

But despite her own heartbreak, she had to be happy about one thing. The fact that her son was developing a very real relationship with his father. That knowledge was doing her heart a lot of good.

As Nigel had said, Kwame was the most important person right now. He was the one that had to come first.

Callie agreed, and she was happy for her son.

She hoped the happiness for her son would be enough to help heal her broken heart.

Chapter 18

Callie told Nigel that she was going to be visiting a friend for a few days at the most, and asked if he wouldn't mind keeping Kwame during that time. Nigel's response been a resounding "No problem." In fact, Callie detected a hint of pride on his face as he'd answered, as if he was happy that she was trusting him to act at Kwame's sole guardian in her absence.

And perhaps Nigel would prefer it this way, a few days for just him and Kwame to hang out. It was fine with her.

And in a few days, she would come back and straighten out her life. Marriage to Nigel would not be a part of her future—she was adamant that she wouldn't settle, no matter how much she wanted to provide Kwame with a traditional family life. But she needed to figure out whether she would stay in Cleveland so that Nigel and his son could be together all the time, or whether she would return to Miami and work out a fair custody arrangement with Nigel.

Yes, Kwame was the most important one to consider in

this situation, but Callie's needs were also important. She had a great career in Florida, one she didn't want to give up. If there was a way to give Kwame all he needed while taking her needs into account as well, she'd certainly take that path.

The decision would have been easy if Nigel had been able to tell her that he loved her. But now…she was going to do what was best for her son *and* for her.

Callie went online and searched flight options. There was a three-thirty flight on United, with one stop, that would get her to Tallahassee by seven-thirty. She would rent a car and drive to Tamara's address. Her arm wasn't one hundred percent, but she could handle driving for half an hour or so.

A short while later, she joined Kwame and Nigel in the living room, where they were playing Dance Central on the Xbox Kinect. Nigel had been trying to keep up with the character on the screen, but stopped when he saw her.

Kwame came right over to her and hugged her. "Dad says you're going away for a few days."

"That's right. How do you feel about staying here with him?"

Kwame met her gaze, smiling. "I think we're gonna have a lot of fun."

"I think so, too." She returned his smile. "So you're not upset that I'm leaving?"

Kwame shrugged. "No. But…"

"But what?"

Kwame didn't speak, just looked uncomfortable. So Callie took him by the hand and led him to her bedroom. "What were you going to say?" she asked. "If you have any concern about staying here with Nigel—"

"It's not about me staying with Dad. It's…I heard you two arguing earlier. Is that why you're suddenly going away?"

He had heard them? He must have come into the house for a moment, even though he'd been playing with Nathan.

Callie hugged Kwame. "No, sweetie. That's not why I'm going away. Tamara…well, she needs me right now. I'm going to help her."

"Are you going to marry Dad?" Kwame suddenly asked.

Callie's mouth fell open. She wanted to speak, but she had no clue what to say.

So she asked her own question. "Do you want me to marry your father?"

Kwame nodded tentatively. "I like being a family."

Callie hugged Kwame again, closing her eyes tightly as she did. Her heart hurt for what she knew would never be.

As much as she loved her son, she couldn't settle simply for his sake. But she wished more than anything that Nigel loved her, and that they could provide the traditional family unit her son so craved.

Who was she kidding? She had always craved such a unit, ever since she was a young girl.

"I've got to get ready for my flight," Callie told him. "I just wanted to make sure you were okay with me leaving. If you want to spend time with your aunts, just call them. And of course, you know you can call me at any time if you want to talk."

"I know."

Taking Kwame's hand in hers, Callie exited the bedroom so she could update Nigel. She didn't quite meet his eyes as she said, "I've just booked a flight for three-thirty. I'm going to quickly pack a few outfits, then I'll call for a taxi to—"

"Don't be silly. I'll take you to the airport."

"Yeah!" Kwame exclaimed, sounding as excited as if they had just booked a trip to Disney. "Dad and I will take you to the airport."

A lump formed in Callie's throat. With each passing moment, her life was getting more complicated. How would

Kwame react if she told him that they were going to head back to Florida, and he would see his father only occasionally?

She couldn't worry about that now. Now, she had to put Nigel out of her mind and deal with Tamara's situation. Indeed, a few days away from her life would hopefully help her come back with a better perspective.

Two hours later, Nigel dropped her off at the airport, and Callie was certain that she saw a glint in her son's eyes. He seemed quite content with the fact that he and his father would have a few days alone together as men, without his mother around.

Again, Callie felt emotion swell in her throat. On one level, things were working out so well for her son and his father that it was such a shame it wasn't working out for her and his father as well.

But once seated on her flight, she forced herself to put thoughts of Nigel and family out of her mind, and instead concentrated on Tamara's plight.

Because if she didn't think about something else, Callie would be consumed with thoughts of all she had lost.

Callie arrived at the house in Tallahassee within twenty minutes of leaving the airport. The evening sky had turned to dusk, but she was thankful that it wasn't dark outside.

She parked her rental vehicle and hurried out. As she made her way to the front door, she noticed there was an SUV in the driveway, one she didn't recognize. Perhaps Tamara had rented a different car. If so, that was a smart thing to do.

Callie rang the doorbell. Then she waited.

Sixty seconds passed with no response. She was filled with a sense of unease, but she tried to ignore it. Certainly there was no cause for concern.

She rang the doorbell a second time, and to make sure she was heard, she also pounded on the door.

At least another thirty seconds passed, and Callie's unease turned into panic. What if something had happened? What if Patrick had shown up since the time Callie and Tamara had spoken and done the unthinkable to her friend?

Callie tried the doorknob, prepared to kick the door down or break a window to get inside. But surprisingly, she found that the door was unlocked.

No sooner than she pushed the door open, she saw Tamara standing there.

Callie gasped, and Tamara did the same, the two of them having startled each other. But the next instant, Callie was flooded with relief. She had started to fear the worst.

"What's going on?" Callie asked. "Are you okay?"

"Yeah. I'm fine," Tamara told her, but her eyes were shifty, and Callie's concern grew.

"He contacted you again?" Callie surmised. "Did you talk to him? Does he know where you are?"

Tamara opened her mouth to speak, and Callie was already thinking that they should be calling 9-1-1. She had a bad feeling. Not even stepping into the house, she reached into her purse and found her BlackBerry. But no sooner than she did, the door opened wide.

And there stood Patrick.

He grinned, but the look held evil, not warmth. "If it isn't the woman who's trying to destroy my marriage."

Prickles of fear spread through Callie's body. Her instincts had told her that something was off, and they had been right.

"Patrick—"

He advanced, and Callie's words got caught in her throat.

"You have messed with my marriage for the last time," Patrick told her. His thick hand wrapped around her neck. As he squeezed, he raised his fist.

And that was the last thing Callie remembered.

Chapter 19

Callie had an odd sensation as her eyelids fluttered, trying to open. It was a sensation of confusion and disorientation.

Where was she?

She heard a steady beeping sound, and her heart rate began to accelerate. She knew something was wrong.

Forcing her eyes open, they slowly came into focus. White. That was what she saw. White all around her, nearly blinding in its intensity. Once again, she closed her eyes.

Then she heard the words, "Oh, thank God."

That voice…Tamara's voice.

Opening her eyes, Callie let them adjust to the light in the room. "Yes, that's it," Tamara said. "Fight to stay awake."

Callie turned her head to the left, and Tamara came into focus. Tamara was sitting beside her, her hands clasped beneath her chin as if she'd been praying.

Again, confusion assailed her.

"I was so worried," Tamara said. "We both were."

Tamara turned then, looking to her right. Callie followed her line of sight, and saw that Tamara's son, Michael was standing against a wall. That was when Callie noticed the heart monitoring machine. Her eyes tracking the steady rise and fall of the green line, alarm gripped her.

Realization hit her. She was in the hospital.

And then it all came back. Being at the house in Tallahassee. Ringing the doorbell. Patrick coming to the door. Patrick grabbing her by the neck and raising his fist.

"What happened?" Callie asked. "What did Patrick do to me?"

Clearly he had hurt her badly enough to land her in the hospital.

"Oh, God," Tamara said, a choked sob following her words. "I'm so sorry. He called me, and I was just so afraid he would hurt someone else I cared about that I told him where I was. I know you said I shouldn't, but I thought…I thought I could work it out. And I think he was close to figuring it out anyway, because he wasn't more than an hour away. I know I should have called you to tell you that he was at the house, but I really didn't think it was an issue anymore. He was acting so much differently. Calmer. Nicer. He seemed happy to be with me again, and I thought I'd made the right decision. But then he saw you…he saw you and he freaked out."

Callie had a flash of a memory of what had happened, and she raised a hand to her forehead. She felt the bandage there. Yes—she had sustained some sort of head trauma again. But how bad it was, she didn't know.

It was daylight outside. Callie asked, "How long have I been here?"

"Since last night," Tamara said. And then she paused. A tear fell down her face. "I've never been so afraid in all of my life."

"Where is he now?" That was what Callie was concerned about. She didn't care if Tamara didn't testify against him, because she would. She may not have been able to identify him as the driver who had forced her off the road, but she had him cold as the man who'd assaulted her.

Callie was tired of the Patricks of the world using and abusing people and getting away with it.

"He was arrested," Tamara said softly.

"Really?" Callie was surprised Patrick had stayed around long enough to let the police capture him. "How?"

Tamara's eyes went toward her son, and she smiled softly. "When Patrick attacked you, Michael came out of nowhere. He had a frying pan. And he just started hitting Patrick, hitting him until he stopped hurting you. I mean, Patrick was beating on you really bad." Tamara gestured to Michael, whose eyes had been downcast the entire time. "Come here, son."

"I just wanted him to stop," Michael said as he came to stand beside his mother.

"You're a hero," Callie told him, hoping to help alleviate any guilt he might feel.

"That's right," Tamara concurred. "You're a hero. I have no doubt that you saved Callie's life." She affectionately patted her son's hand, and he smiled for the first time.

"Thank you," Callie said. "You were very brave."

"He won't be hurting you again," Tamara said. "Nor me. He won't be hurting anyone. His bail has been revoked, so he'll be in jail until his trial."

"You have no reason to fear testifying against him," Callie said. "And I'm going to testify against him, as well. This latest assault is going to guarantee that he goes away for a long, long time."

Tamara nodded, but there was sadness in her eyes. Callie could only imagine that this was a bittersweet moment for

her friend. Despite the happiness that Patrick had been apprehended, Tamara had to have some regrets. The biggest was
no doubt the regret that the person she had loved had turned
out to be such a monster.

Callie's mind ventured to her own situation, to just how
stark the contrast between Nigel and Patrick was. Patrick had
never wanted to be separated from Tamara, in part claiming
he didn't want to be out of his son's life, but he had hardly
been an ideal father. Nigel, on the other hand, had not been
involved in his son's life through no fault of his own but
had stepped up to the plate to be the father he knew Kwame
needed him to be.

It was a huge part of why Callie loved him. And yet she
had run from him for far less substantial reasons than Tamara
had run from Patrick.

"I hope you don't mind that I called your family in Cleveland," Tamara said. "Nigel and Kwame are on their way."

Callie's eyes widened as she looked at Tamara, and her
heart pounded against her chest. "You did?"

Tamara nodded. "I did. I felt they needed to know. I called
your uncle, and he said he'd call Nigel and Kwame, but I asked
for the number so I could do it myself. I felt I owed Kwame
that."

Good Lord, how worried her son must be. "What did
Kwame say?"

"He just wanted to know if you were okay, that was the
only thing he asked. I told him you were going to be fine, but
that you'd been badly hurt."

"My poor baby. To get a phone call like that."

"He took the news better than Nigel did."

At the mention of Nigel, Callie's stomach fluttered.
"What—what did Nigel say?"

"He was flustered, that's for sure. Grilled me about what
had happened, where Patrick was now, and of course, where

you were. He even called the hospital and spoke to the physician about you."

"He did?" Callie asked, her lips curling into a small smile. How silly she was, feeling a measure of happiness that Nigel had been so concerned.

"He said he was going to get on a flight immediately, but when I pointed out the time, he contemplated driving. Ultimately, I told him that a flight in the morning would be the best thing—faster, safer. I expect he'll be here shortly."

Again, Callie's stomach fluttered. Was Nigel simply a man who was concerned about her as a friend? Or did his concern mean something more?

Even now, she held out hope that he would love her completely, as he once had. Amazing how hard it was to let go of that dream.

Callie couldn't help remembering Nigel's words. He'd said to her that she had offered him no guarantees that she wouldn't run again. She had figured that giving herself to him—body and soul—should have made her feelings clear. But suddenly she was seeing his position in a different light.

The fact that he had even opened himself up to her had shown that he *did* care. Time, distance and their complicated history had likely changed him. The Nigel she had known ten years ago wasn't afraid to share his feelings, but could Callie blame him for guarding his heart, if that's what he was doing? He was afraid, too. Afraid because she had left him once before.

And the fact that Callie had faced death once again— knowing that she might never have seen her son one more time, nor the man she loved—was beyond sobering.

When she saw Nigel, she would lay her heart on the line. She hadn't really done that for him. And she knew why— having been abandoned by her mother, she didn't trust people.

She tended to close herself off before she could get hurt. To push people away before they could push her away.

Had she really been that different with Nigel this time around? Seeing him again had been about him getting to know his son, but the unexpected had happened. Her relationship with Nigel had reignited. She had allowed herself to feel what she was feeling, and the passion had been exquisite. But had anything changed on her part to assure Nigel that this time she wouldn't leave?

The very fact that he had proposed marriage spoke volumes…but hearing him say that he loved her would still be exactly what she wanted.

She had considered heading back to Florida to resume her job, and having Kwame see Nigel regularly throughout the year. But suddenly, she wondered if that sort of part-time parenthood would be good enough. She wasn't certain if marriage was the best answer, but having deprived Nigel of Kwame for so many years of his life, didn't she owe it to him to relocate to Cleveland to allow Nigel to be a real father to his son?

Tamara looked toward Michael and said, "Son, do you mind going to the cafeteria and picking up a couple of orange juices or apple juice?"

"Sure," he said.

Tamara gave him a few dollars—and a hug—and then Michael left the room. Once he was gone, Tamara looked at her friend and said, "Tell me what's going on. I for one was shocked to call Cleveland and learn that Kwame was staying with Nigel. I see there's a lot you haven't filled me in on."

"I'm not sure there's anything to tell."

Tamara frowned. "Uh-oh. It's complicated, isn't it?"

"Kinda sorta."

"You know you can tell me anything. You're my best friend."

So Callie told her. Told her about how she and Nigel had reunited, how Nigel had fit into their life perfectly, that Kwame especially was elated to know his father. "And then he proposed," Callie concluded.

Tamara's eyes lit up. "He proposed? That's wonderful!" She paused. "Isn't it?"

"I told him no."

"What?"

"I didn't want to marry him—not if he didn't love me. Because I asked if he loved me, and he couldn't say that he did."

"But this is Nigel," Tamara said. "I know how much you loved him."

"Which is why the decision was so hard. It would have been easier if I had no feelings for him at all. How could I marry him and bear being so close to him, knowing he didn't return my feelings?"

"I sense a but…"

"But now I'm wondering, rethinking everything. Here I am, lying in a hospital bed. I could have been killed. And I know part of that is because I ran the moment I had a chance. You had a problem, and yes I wanted to be there for you, but your problem became a reason for me to run from Nigel once again. Damn him, he was so right to be guarded."

"What exactly are you saying?" Tamara asked.

"He said something to me," Callie explained. "When I asked if he loved me, he said I'd given him no guarantee that I was in it for the long haul. Of course, I was thinking why should I marry him unless he gave *me* a guarantee…but I see now that he had every reason to distrust me. I ran again—the first moment I could."

"Did *you* tell him that you love him?" Tamara asked.

"I…" Callie's voice trailed off as she thought of the answer. Good Lord, she hadn't. She had hoped—expected—that Nigel would tell her that he loved her, but she hadn't told him that herself. She had shown him, but what if that wasn't enough? What if that wasn't enough for a man whom she had hurt probably more than anyone could ever hurt him?

"I didn't," Callie said softly. "I just thought…I thought he would know."

"Why—because he's psychic?" Tamara challenged.

"Oh God…" Callie's voice trailed off once again as she thought of the gravity of the situation.

"You're not the only one who needs reassurance, now are you?" Tamara asked. "All I can say is this. If Patrick was half the man that Nigel appears to be, I wouldn't hesitate to marry him. And if we had the kind of love you two had? Heck, it'd be a no-brainer."

At the sound of the soft knocking, Callie looked in the direction of the door. She figured Tamara and Michael were returning from having their snack, but instead, she saw Nigel and Kwame appear as the door slowly opened.

"Mommy!" Kwame exclaimed, and ran straight toward her. Callie giggled as she thought he was about to throw himself onto her, not caring if she felt any physical pain. Just seeing her son again was the kind of medicine she needed.

But Kwame stopped short of that, and instead leaned over her and hugged her as gently as he could.

"Oh, my baby," Callie said and kissed the top of his head. Her eyes misted at the thought that things could have played out very differently for her son. What if she had left him without a mother?

Kwame eased backward and sat in the chair beside the bed. Callie looked toward the door at Nigel, who appeared to be waiting for her and Kwame to have their moment before entering. Then, holding her gaze, he slowly entered the room.

Callie's breath caught in her throat at the sight of him, at his strong, sexy movements. She wondered if she would ever tire of seeing him. If that rush that came with the first glimpse of him would ever get old.

She knew that it would not.

She saw something on his face that caused all the air to leave her lungs in a rush. Because it was more than mere concern. He was scared.

"We came as soon as we could," Nigel said.

Callie nodded. "I—I'm sorry I put you both through this. Especially Kwame. He must've been terrified."

"He wasn't the only one worried," Nigel said, giving her a pointed look.

"Of course not. I didn't mean that the way it sounded. Sorry."

"Don't apologize," Nigel told her. "Tamara filled me in, and I know you were trying to help out your friend. I also know that Patrick will never be a problem again. If he weren't caught, I would hunt him down myself and make sure that he never laid another hand on you or any other person."

There was something utterly sexy about a man when he made it clear, without a doubt, that he would always protect you.

"Thankfully, both Tamara and I are safe from him."

"And for that, Kwame and I are both grateful. Trust me, when Tamara called and told me that you'd been rushed to the hospital, I was terrified."

Callie looked at Nigel, and saw in him all the man she had ever wanted, or could ever want.

He had embraced fatherhood in a wholehearted way, completing Kwame's life. And as much as he could have been upset with her—and no doubt he had been—he let none of that affect his relationship with his son.

"Kwame, will you give me and your father a moment?"

Kwame stared at her a few seconds before answering. Then he nodded. "Okay."

Once he left the room, Nigel spoke. "Our argument yesterday—"

"Shh," Callie interjected. "I need to speak first, get something off my chest. You said something to me before I left, when we had our argument. You pointed out that while you hadn't said that you loved me, I hadn't given you any reassurances that I would not take off again.

"I realize now that I've been holding my heart so close to my chest because I didn't want to get hurt. But in doing so, I didn't give you what you needed. I don't know if you'll ever love me again, but I want you to know that I love you.

"I walked away from you years ago because I was afraid. Not because of anything you said or did, but because I was scared to death that you wouldn't love me forever. My own mother didn't…" Callie's voice cracked, and she stopped.

"Even now, I'm still afraid. But I'm going to put my heart on the line and tell you how deeply I feel for you. And I know you might reject me, and that terrifies me. But I can't live my life being afraid anymore.

"Seeing you with Kwame has made me realize that perhaps if I hadn't been so scared, I would've had the life I'd always wanted all along. I threw it away. I have no one to blame but myself." Callie paused and reached for Nigel's hand.

"And if you don't think you can ever love me again, I—I'll have to be okay with that. Because what you've done for our son…" Her voice trailed off, and she actually choked back a sob.

Then Nigel was stroking her cheek, and she raised her gaze to meet his once more. He was looking at her with an expression she had seen so many times when they'd been together ten years ago. And it was unmistakable.

It was love.

"When I asked you before what you regretted about leaving me and all you said was that you regretted taking my son away from me, I wondered if you would ever stop running from your fears. Because I knew that's what made you run the first time. And indeed, the only reason that I've been able to feel love for you again is because I know deep in your heart you were just so afraid, so unable to believe and trust in love because of your mother."

Callie's heart filled with hope. "Did you say you love me?"

"I don't think I ever stopped loving you," Nigel explained. "I had serious doubts about whether or not we could have a relationship again, especially not if you were guarding your heart the same way you did back then. But damn, Callie—" His lips curled in a slow smile. "You're the only woman who's ever had my heart."

Callie reached for his shirt and pulled him toward her while lifting her own head toward his. She planted her mouth on his and kissed him. Reluctantly, she broke the kiss, saying, "Oh, Nigel. You don't know how happy that makes me. I thought I had ruined my chances with you forever."

"One thing I've learned where you're concerned," Nigel began, "is that I can't get you out of my heart. Even if I want to. Make no mistake, when we made love, it was because I still love you. Even if the next morning I gave myself the lecture that I'd be foolish to give you my heart again."

Callie squeezed Nigel's hand.

"I should have laid my heart on the line then," he went on. "But like you, I was afraid."

"We've both made mistakes," Callie said, "but we're here now. That's what matters."

Nigel raised her hand to his lips and kissed it. "I have something to tell you."

Was he going to propose to her now, in earnest? "Yes, sweetheart?"

Nigel beamed. "Damn, I love the way you call me sweetheart."

"Get used to it. Because I'm going to be doing it for the rest of my life."

Nigel stroked her forehead. "As my wife. In the real sense of the word. Because that's the only reason I proposed. Because I love you. You're the only woman I've ever wanted to mar—"

Callie placed a finger on his lips to silence him. "I know. And yes, I'll be your wife."

He kissed her again, and sighed as he pulled apart. "If we keep this up, I'm going to forget what I want to tell you."

Even in a hospital room, Callie was getting turned on by him. She had no doubt that Nigel was the man she was supposed to spend her life with.

"Okay," she said. "What do you want to tell me?"

"It's about your mother."

Callie's heart began to accelerate. "My mom?"

"I've got a very good lead on where she was last. She was living—as far as I know—in Philadelphia. I've got a lead that we can follow, and hopefully we'll find her."

"Are you serious?"

"I would never joke about this. I know how much this means to you."

"And *you* mean everything to me," she told him, and then, slipping her arms around Nigel's neck, she kissed him again.

A kiss that showed him that she was no longer holding back.

And a kiss that proved to her that when you let down the walls around your heart, the sweetest of rewards awaits you.

* * * * *

REQUEST YOUR FREE BOOKS!

2 FREE NOVELS
PLUS 2 FREE GIFTS!

KIMANI ROMANCE ™

Love's ultimate destination!